But now he realised that which made her figure, thir undeniable enticement, and that her big eyes filling her small, pale face were beautiful rather differently from the way he had interpreted beauty in the past.

All his women had been, he thought, like full-grown roses, big-breasted, seductive, voluptuous, and in contrast Giselda was the exact opposite.

Arrow Books by Barbara Cartland

AUTOBIOGRAPHY
I Search for Rainbows
We Danced All Night
Polly: the Story of My Wonderful Mother
Josephine Empress of France

ROMANTIC NOVELS

Barbara Cartland

THE MYSTERIOUS
MAID-SERVANT

ARROW BOOKS

Arrow Books Ltd
3 Fitzroy Square, London WIP 6JD

An imprint of the Hutchinson Publishing Group

London Melbourne Sydney Auckland
Wellington Johannesburg and agencies
throughout the world

First published by Hutchinson & Co (Publishers) Ltd 1977
Arrow edition 1978
© Barbara Cartland 1977

Made and printed in Great Britain
by The Anchor Press Ltd
Tiptree, Essex

ISBN 0 09 918270 X

Author's Note

The descriptions of Cheltenham in 1816 are all accurate. The Montpellier Pump Room was pulled down and rebuilt the following year. The Weighing-Machine from Williams' Library is in the Museum.

The Duke of Wellington paid three more visits to Cheltenham in the post-war years, but later he had some competition as in 1823 the visitors included 'four Dukes, three Duchesses, six Marquises, ten Earls, fifty-three Lords and seventy Ladies!'

The Duc d'Orléans stayed for three months and later became Louis Philippe, King of France.

Colonel Berkeley lived with Maria Foote for several years. She bore him two children.

Always flamboyant in his behaviour, when the Editor of the *Cheltenham Chronicle* criticised his conduct he was furious, and when the newspaper went on to make uncomplimentary remarks about the ladies of the Berkeley Hunt, the Colonel with two friends proceeded to the Editor's house. While his friends guarded the door the Colonel horse-whipped the wretched man.

But Colonel Berkeley was a great benefactor to the town. He helped start the Cheltenham Races and he was later made Lord Seagrave and then Earl Fitzhardinge.

Berkeley Castle is still one of the most beautiful Castles in England. To find money for its preservation and to restore it to its former grandeur, Berkeley Square and the estate in the heart of Mayfair were sold in 1919.

Thomas Newell became Surgeon Extraordinary to King George IV.

1816

1

'Damn and blast! God Almighty! You curst fool – take your clumsy hands off me! Get out – do you hear? You are sacked – and I never want to see your ugly face again!'

The valet ran from the room and the occupant of the bed went on cursing volubly with soldier's oaths that came easily to his lips.

Then as he felt his rage abating a little he saw a movement at the far end of the big bedroom and realised for the first time that a maid-servant was attending to the grate.

She had been obscured from his view by the carved foot of the big four-poster bed, and now he raised himself a little higher on his pillows to say:

'Who are you? What are you doing here? I did not realise there was anyone else in the room.'

She turned and he saw that she was very slight and her face seemed unnaturally small beneath a large mob-cap.

'I . . I was polishing the . . grate My Lord.'

To his surprise her voice was soft and cultured, and the Earl stared at her as she moved towards the door, a heavy brass bucket in one hand.

'Come here!' he said abruptly.

She hesitated a moment. Then as if she forced herself to obey his command she walked slowly towards the bed, and he saw she was even younger than he had first imagined.

She stopped at the bedside, but when he would have spoken she stared down at his leg exposed above the knee,

7

and at the blood-stained bandages which the valet had been in the process of removing.

The Earl was about to speak when she said, again in that soft but undoubtedly educated voice:

'Would you .. allow me to remove the bandages for you? I have some experience of nursing.'

The Earl looked at her in surprise, then said ungraciously:

'You could not hurt me more than that damned fool I have just driven out of my sight.'

The maid drew a little nearer and putting down the heavy bucket she stood looking at the Earl's leg. Then very gently she moved a piece of the bandage to one side.

'I am afraid, My Lord, that the lint which has been covering the wounds was not properly applied. It is therefore stuck, and will undoubtedly be painful unless we can ease it off with warm water.'

'Do what you like!' the Earl said gruffly, 'and I will try to restrain my language.'

'Forget I am a woman, My Lord. My father said a man who could endure pain without swearing was either a saint or a turnip!'

The Earl's lips twisted in a faint smile.

He watched her as the maid went to the wash-hand-stand.

Having first washed her hands in cold water she emptied the basin into a slop-pail. Then she poured some of the hot water with which his valet had intended to shave him into the china basin.

She brought it to the side of the bed and with some cottonwool which had been lying on a table she began deftly to ease away with the soaked wool the bandages where they had stuck to the innumerable scars that had been left by the Surgeon after he had removed the grape-shot from the Earl of Lyndhurst's leg.

He had been shot at close range immediately above the

knee and it was only by a tremendous effort of will and because he used all his authority as a General that his leg had not been amputated immediately after the Battle of Waterloo.

'It'll become gangrenous, My Lord,' the Surgeon had protested, 'and then Your Lordship will lose not your leg, but your life!'

'I will take a chance on it,' the Earl had replied. 'I am damned if I will go through life "dot-and-carry-one", unable to mount a horse in comfort.'

'I'm warning Your Lordship . .'

'And I am disregarding your warning, and rejecting your very debatable skill,' the Earl replied.

It had however been some months before he could be brought home to England on a stretcher in considerable pain.

After enduring what he considered indifferent treatment in London, he had come to Cheltenham because he had heard that the Surgeon at the Spa, Thomas Newell, was outstanding.

The Earl was indeed one of the many hundreds of people who visited Cheltenham entirely because of its exceptional doctors.

Although Thomas Newell had made his Lordship suffer more agony than he had ever encountered in the whole of his life, his faith in him was justified; for there was no doubt that the scars on the leg were in a healthy condition and beginning to heal.

He did not swear again, even though he winced once or twice as the maid removed the last of the blood-stained lint and looked around for fresh bandages.

'On top of the chest-of-drawers,' the Earl prompted.

The maid found a box containing bandages and some lint which she looked at critically.

'What is wrong?' the Earl enquired.

'There is nothing wrong, except that there is nothing to prevent the lint from sticking to the wounds just as

9

what I have removed did. If Your Lordship will permit me, I will bring you an ointment my mother makes which is not only healing but also will prevent the lint from sticking.'

'I should be glad to receive the ointment,' the Earl replied.

'I will bring it tomorrow,' she said.

Having arranged the pieces of lint on the wound, she secured them in place with strips of clean linen.

'Why must I wait until tomorrow?' the Earl enquired.

'I cannot go home until my work is done.'

'What is your work?'

'I am a housemaid.'

'You have been here long?'

'I came here yesterday.'

The Earl glanced at the brass bucket on the floor beside the bed.

'I imagine you have been given the roughest and heaviest jobs,' he said. 'You do not look as if you are capable of carrying such a heavy burden.'

'I can manage.'

The words were spoken with a note of determination in the maid's voice which told him that what she had had to do up to now had not been easy.

Then as he watched her fingers moving deftly on his leg the Earl was suddenly arrested by the bones of her wrists.

There was something prominent about them, something which commanded his attention and made him look even more searchingly at her face.

It was difficult to see her clearly, for her head was bent and the mob-cap obstructed his view.

Then as she turned to choose another bandage he saw that her face was very thin, unnaturally so, the cheekbones prominent, the chin-bone taut, the mouth stretched at the corners.

As if she realised she was being scrutinised, her eyes

met his and he thought they were too large for her small face.

They were strange eyes, the deep blue of an angry sea, fringed with long eyelashes.

She looked at him enquiringly, then a faint colour rose in her cheeks as she continued to apply the bandages.

The Earl looked again at the prominent bones of her wrists and knew when he had seen them last.

It was the children in Portugal, the children of the peasants whose crops had been destroyed! They had been left starving by the warring armies who lived off the land and who, especially the French, left nothing for the native population.

Starvation!

It had sickened and disgusted him, even though he knew it was one of the inevitable horrors of war. He had seen too much of it to be mistaken now.

He realised that while he was thinking of the maid she had finished bandaging his leg with a skill that his valet had been unable to command.

Now she pulled the sheet gently over him and picked up her coal-bucket.

'Wait!' the Earl said. 'I asked you a question, which you have not yet answered. Who are you?'

'My name is Giselda, My Lord .. Giselda .. Chart.'

There was just a slight hesitation before the last name which the Earl did not miss.

'This is not the type of work to which you are accustomed?'

'No, My Lord, but I am grateful to have it.'

'Your family is poor?'

'Very poor, My Lord.'

'What does it consist of?'

'My mother and my small brother.'

'Your father is dead?'

'Yes, My Lord.'

'Then how have you lived until you came here?'

He had a feeling that Giselda was resenting his questions, and yet she was not in a position to refuse to answer them.

She stood holding the brass bucket which was so heavy that it pulled her body down on one side, making her seem too fragile and too unsubstantial for such a heavy weight.

Now the Earl could see the hollows at the base of her neck beneath the neat collar of her print dress and the sharp points of her elbows.

She was suffering from starvation – he was sure of it – and he knew the whiteness of her skin was a pallor that indicated anaemia.

'Put down that bucket while I talk to you,' he said sharply.

She obeyed him, her eyes wide and apprehensive in her face, as if she was afraid of what he was about to say.

'It is a waste of your talents, Giselda,' he said after a moment, 'to be polishing grates and doubtless scrubbing floors, when your fingers have healing powers.'

Giselda did not move or answer, she merely waited as the Earl went on:

'I am going to suggest to the Housekeeper that you wait exclusively upon me.'

'I do not think she will allow that, My Lord. They are short-handed below, which is the reason why I was able to obtain employment here. The town is filling up because of the opening of the new Assembly Rooms.'

'I am not concerned with the Housekeeper's problems,' the Earl said loftily. 'If I want you and she will not agree, I will take you into my own employment.'

He paused.

'Perhaps that would be better anyway. I require you to bandage my leg twice a day, and there will be doubtless many other services you can render me which a woman can do more effectively than a man.'

'I am .. very grateful to Your Lordship .. but .. I would rather refuse.'

'Refuse? Why should you wish to do that?' the Earl asked.

'Because, My Lord, I cannot risk losing the employment I have here.'

'Risk? What risk is there?'

'I would not wish to be .. dismissed as you dismissed your valet just now.'

The Earl laughed.

'If you imagine I have dismissed Batley you are very much mistaken! Even if I meant it, I doubt if he would go. He has been with me for fifteen years and he is used to the rough edge of my tongue. I will try to be more careful where you are concerned.'

Giselda linked her fingers together and looked at the Earl even more apprehensively than she had done before.

'What is troubling you now?' he asked. 'I cannot believe that you would not find nursing me more congenial than being ordered about by a horde of servants.'

'It is not .. that .. My Lord.'

'Then what is it?'

'I was wondering what .. remuneration you would .. give me.'

'What are you receiving now?'

'Ten shillings a week, My Lord. It is a good wage, but it is well known that they pay well here at German Cottage. I might not get the same elsewhere.'

'Ten shillings?' the Earl said. 'Well, I will give you double.'

He saw the look of surprise light the dark blue eyes, and he thought too that there was a sudden gleam of excitement in them.

Then Giselda's chin went up and she said:

'I have no wish to accept charity, My Lord.'

'Although you need it,' the Earl remarked dryly.

Again the colour rose in her thin cheeks and he added:

'Is there no other money coming into your home except for what you are bringing in?'

'N . No, My Lord.'

'Then how have you been living until now?'

'My mother .. embroiders very skilfully .. but unfortunately her fingers have stiffened and so for the moment she cannot .. work.'

'Then you will accept a pound a week from me.'

There was again a definite hesitation before Giselda replied:

'Thank you .. My Lord.'

'You will take a week's wages now,' the Earl said. 'There is a guinea in the top right-hand drawer of the chest. You will then change into your ordinary clothes and have luncheon with me before you go home and fetch me that ointment which you spoke of.'

'H . have .. luncheon with you, My Lord?'

'That is what I said.'

'But it would not be .. right, My Lord.'

'Why not?'

'I .. am a .. servant, My Lord.'

'Good God! Are you trying to teach me etiquette?' the Earl exclaimed. 'A Nanny may lunch with her charges, a Tutor may lunch with his pupils, and if I require the woman who is nursing me to eat at my bedside, then she will do as she is told!'

'Yes .. My Lord.'

'Follow my instructions and send the Housekeeper to me immediately. I will see Batley first. I expect you will find him outside.'

Giselda gave the Earl a quick glance, then picked up the brass bucket. She did not look at him but went out closing the door quietly behind her.

The Earl leant back against his pillows. There was some mystery here and he liked a mystery.

Batley came in a moment after the door had closed.

'I am engaging that young woman as my nurse, Batley,' the Earl said.

'I hope she proves satisfactory, M'Lord,' Batley replied.

He was speaking in the repressed, offended voice which he always used after the Earl had cursed him, but they both knew it was little more than play-acting.

'She is no ordinary maid-servant, Batley,' the Earl went on.

'No, M'Lord. I realised that yesterday, when I saw her downstairs.'

'Where does she come from?'

'I'll try to find out, M'Lord. But I imagines as they'll know little. They're short-handed and the Colonel likes his household full at all times.'

That was true, the Earl knew.

Colonel Berkeley, who was his host and who owned German Cottage, was a man who expected perfection and created hell if he did not get it.

The uncrowned King of Cheltenham, William Fitzhardinge Berkeley was the oldest son of the Fifth Earl.

He had sat in the House of Commons six years earlier in 1810 as one of the Members for the County of Gloucester, but he resigned his seat on the death of his father when he expected to enter the House of Lords as the Sixth Earl of Berkeley.

His claim to the Earldom, however, was not sustained on the grounds that the marriage of his parents had not taken place until after the birth of their first three sons.

The Dowager Lady Berkeley however convinced her fourth son Moreton, who was in fact her eighth child, that this decision was wrong and he refused to accept the title or the property.

Colonel Berkeley, as he continued to be called – Fitz to his family and friends – therefore was treated as head of the family, the owner of Berkeley Castle and the family estates.

A tall, handsome man, Colonel Berkeley was also a

martinet, an autocrat and, where Cheltenham was concerned, a tyrant.

The Spa was his hobby and he lavished his time and his wealth upon the place where his utterances and his flamboyant, tempestuous way of life were a constant source of gossip and excitement both to the townsfolk and to the visitors.

Not that he cared what was said. He was a law unto himself, and no party was a success without him. Riots, dinners, Assemblies and theatrical performances were arranged to suit his convenience.

Being a bachelor he was desired as a son-in-law by every scheming mother, but he had no intention of sacrificing his freedom until he was ready to do so.

Therefore German Cottage, in which the Earl was staying at present, had entertained many beautiful and glamorous visitors who were intimately connected with the Colonel, but did not wear his ring on their third finger.

The Earl had met the Colonel in the hunting field and they had become close friends with a common interest in sport.

Colonel Berkeley, who had his own pack of Harriers at the age of sixteen, now at thirty hunted his hounds in the Cotswold and Berkeley country alternately.

He had made the Berkeley Hunt Staff abandon their historic tawny coats and instead wear a scarlet coat with a black velvet collar having a flying fox embroidered thereon in silver and gold.

The Colonel was very popular as a Master and was always ready to pay liberally for poultry destroyed or any damage done by his hounds.

At the moment he was at the Castle which was why the Earl was staying alone at German Cottage, but the twenty-five minutes from Berkeley to Cheltenham meant nothing to him and he would ride far further when he was hunting.

It was the fashion in Cheltenham to refer to the magnificent and impressive mansions with which the town abounded, as 'cottages'.

They were in fact nothing of the sort, and the Earl found the luxury with which he was surrounded very much to his taste.

He was well aware that the best Hotel, which was 'The Plough', would not have provided him with anything like the comfort he could enjoy as the Colonel's guest.

It did not strike him in the least reprehensible that he should steal one of his host's servants because he required her services for himself.

He sent for the Housekeeper and told her of his plans. Because the woman was used to the ways of her master and found the 'Quality' invariably incomprehensible in their behaviour, she merely curtsied and told the Earl that although it would be difficult she would try to find some-one else to replace Giselda.

'Why difficult?' the Earl enquired.

'Girls are not always willing to work at the Castle or house,' Mrs Kingdom replied.

The Earl remembered that one of his friend's preoccupations was the begetting of more illegitimate Berkeleys. He had been told that there were thirty-three within a radius of ten miles of the Castle.

It was therefore all the more surprising that Giselda should be working at German Cottage, but he fancied she was not aware of her employer's reputation.

'What do you know about the girl?' the Earl asked the Housekeeper.

'Nothing, M'Lord, but she is nicely spoken and obviously a better class than most of the applicants for the job, which were not many. I took her on hoping she'd turn out satisfactorily.'

'You must have noticed that she seemed rather frail for the type of work to which you assigned her?'

Mrs Kingdom shrugged her shoulders.

She did not say so in so many words, but she implied

that either a domestic servant could do the work, or she could not. In the latter case there was only one remedy – to be rid of her.

The Earl, who was used to dealing with both men and women in his position of command, sensed all that Mrs Kingdom did not say.

'Giselda will by my servant and I will pay her wages,' he said. 'As she does not sleep in the house, she will require a room in which to change her clothes if she wishes to do so.'

'That'll be seen to, M'Lord.'

Mrs Kingdom curtsied politely and left the room.

The Earl shouted for his valet.

'Food, Batley! Where is the food I ordered?'

'It's coming, M'Lord. It's unlike you to eat so early.'

'I will eat when I please,' the Earl said sharply, 'and tell the Butler I want a bottle of decent claret.'

'Very good, M'Lord.'

The Earl watched the two footmen bringing in the table which they set beside his bed. Then they carried in a tray of cold meats which would have stimulated the appetite of an epicure.

Colonel Berkeley, unlike many of his contemporaries, was as interested in food as in drink, and the Earl, when he had been abroad, had learnt to appreciate the more subtle flavours of Continental cooking.

'Tonight I will order a different sort of meal,' he thought.

He realised he was interested in his experiment to see how a starving person would react to a sudden abundance of food.

How often in Portugal he had wished he had a hundred bullock carts full of grain to distribute among the women and children?

But as it was the troops often went hungry and there was nothing to spare.

He had never expected to find starvation in England,

which even after the long years of war with Napoleon seemed to be a land flowing with milk and honey.

Giselda came into the room looking very different from the way she had left it.

She was wearing a plain blue gown which the Earl recognised was slightly old-fashioned. At the same time it was by no means the type of garment that would have been worn by a servant.

A small muslin collar encircled her neck, tied with a bow of blue velvet ribbon, and the same in the shape of small muslin ruffles encircled her wrists.

They hid the prominent bones on her arms, but nothing could disguise the taut lines of her chin, or the shadows beneath her cheek-bones.

Now that she had removed the large mob-cap, the Earl could see that her hair was fair and brushed back from an oval forehead.

It was arranged in imitation of a fashionable style, but he had the feeling that, like its owner, the hair had grown thinner and was limp and lacked buoyancy through lack of nutrition.

She stood just inside the door and after a quick glance at the table and the silver dishes piled high with food she looked only at the Earl.

'I am waiting for you to join me,' he said, 'and because I think under the circumstances you would prefer it we will wait on ourselves – or rather you will wait on me.'

'Yes, My Lord.'

'I would like a glass of claret, and I hope you will join me.'

Giselda lifted the decanter from a side-table and filled the Earl's glass, then she looked at the one which had been set for her and hesitated.

'It will do you good,' the Earl said.

'I think it would be . . unwise, My Lord.'

'Why ?'

Even as he asked the question he knew it was a stupid one, and substituted another.

'When did you last eat?'

'Before I left here yesterday evening.'

'Did you have a big meal?'

'I thought I was hungry, but I found it difficult to swallow.'

The Earl knew this was inevitably the result of malnutrition.

'I suppose you took home what you could not eat?' he remarked in a practical tone.

'I could not do .. that.'

'They would not give you the food?'

'I asked the Chef if I could have a half-chicken which was left from your dinner and which he was about to drop into the waste-bin.'

She paused before she went on:

'He did not answer me. He threw what was left of the chicken to a dog which had already eaten too much to be interested in it.'

She told the story without any emotion in her voice. She was just stating a fact.

'Sit down,' the Earl said. 'I want to see you eat, and let me say before we start that anything that is left you can take home with you.'

He saw Giselda stiffen. Then she said:

'You make me feel ashamed. I was not begging when I told you that story.'

'I had already decided before you told it to me what I intended to do,' the Earl said. 'Now eat, child, and for God's sake stop arguing with me. If there is one thing that infuriates me it is when someone argues about everything I suggest.'

There was just a suspicion of a smile on Giselda's lips as she seated herself.

'I am sorry .. My Lord .. and I am in fact very .. grateful.'

'Then show it by putting some food inside you,' he said. 'I do not like thin women.'

She smiled again.

As he helped himself to a piece of boar's head she took a slice of tongue on to her plate, then waited while she passed the Earl the sauces to embellish the meat he had chosen.

If he had been expecting to enjoy the spectacle of some-one very hungry making up for long weeks of want he was to be disappointed.

Giselda ate slowly and daintily and long before the Earl had finished she could eat no more.

The Earl persuaded her to drink a little claret, but a few sips was all she would touch.

'I have grown used to being without,' she said apologetically, 'but now with the money you have given me we shall fare better.'

'I imagine it will not go far,' the Earl said dryly. 'I am told that prices have increased enormously since the war.'

'That is true, but we will still . . manage.'

'Have you always lived in Cheltenham ?'

'No.'

'Where did you live ?'

'In a small village in . . Worcestershire.'

'Then why have you come into town ?'

There was a moment's silence, then Giselda said :

'If your Lordship will excuse me I would like now to go home and collect the ointment you will need for your leg. I am not certain that my mother has enough. If not she will make some more, and that will take time. I would not wish you to be without it tonight.'

The Earl looked at her.

'In other words, you do not intend to answer my questions !'

'No . . My Lord.'

'Why not ?'

'I would not wish Your Lordship to think me impertinent, but my home life is private.'

'Why?'

'For reasons that I am .. unable to tell .. Your Lordship.'

Her eyes met the Earl's and it seemed as if there was for a moment a battle of wills between them.

Then the Earl said in an exasperated tone:

'Why the hell must you be so secretive and mysterious? I am interested in you, and God knows I have little enough to interest me lying here day after day with nothing but my blasted leg to think about!'

'I am .. sorry that I should .. disappoint Your Lordship.'

'But you do not intend to assuage my curiosity?'

'No .. My Lord.'

The Earl could not help being amused.

It seemed so extraordinary that this frail creature with her thin face and prominent bones should defy him even though she must know that he was prepared to be her benefactor.

However, since for the moment he had no wish to bully her, he gave in with good grace.

'Very well, then, have it your own way. Pack up what you want and be off with you, and do not be late coming back or I shall imagine that you have absconded with my money.'

'You must realise it is always a mistake to pay in advance.'

And although he was surprised at her reply he found himself smiling at it.

She packed the cold meats from the dishes in white paper, folded them neatly into a parcel and picked it up in both hands.

'Thank you very much, My Lord,' she said softly.

Then as if she suddenly recalled herself to her duties she said:

'You will rest this afternoon? And if possible you should sleep.'

'Are you ordering me to do so?'

'Of course! You have put me in the position of nursing you. I must therefore tell Your Lordship what is the right thing to do even if you refuse to do it.'

'Do you anticipate that I might?'

'I think it unlikely that anyone could make you do anything you did not want to do, and I am therefore appealing to Your Lordship's better judgement.'

'That is very astute of you, Giselda,' the Earl said. 'But you know as well as I do that "when the cat is away the mice will play". So, if you care about my well-being, I suggest you are not away for too long.'

'I shall return as soon as I have the ointment, My Lord.'

Giselda curtsied with a grace that was indefinable and went from the room.

The Earl watched her go and picking up his glass of claret drank it reflectively.

For the first time for a year he had an interest outside his own health.

An active man, a man who for the past ten years had been occupied in either the field of battle or the field of sport, he found the inaction imposed upon him since being wounded an intolerable condition.

He violently resented his ill health. It was a weakness he despised, and he fought against it, as if it was an enemy he must wear down and vanquish.

There was no reason for him to be alone.

Cheltenham was full of people who were well aware of his social importance and of officers who had either served under him or who admired him as a military leader.

They would have been only too pleased to visit him and when it was possible, entertain him in their houses.

But the Earl was not only in bad health: he was also bad-tempered. He had been outstandingly fit all his life - and he loathed being now an invalid.

He decided quite unreasonably that society bored him and especially a society where he could not for the moment enjoy the favours of attractive women.

Like his Commander, the Duke of Wellington, the Earl liked the society of women, especially those with whom he could indulge in a freedom of speech and manner that was not permissible in the *Beau Monde*.

His *affaires de cœur* therefore ranged from the Opera Singers at Drury Lane to the most attractive and fashionable beauties of St James'.

It was difficult for any of them to refuse him anything he asked; for he was not only important by birth and extremely rich, he also had that indefinable attraction that women found irresistible.

It was not simply because he was tall, broad-shouldered and handsome, and in uniform made a picture that was enough to make any female's heart beat more quickly; there was in addition something in his manner that women found fascinating.

It captivated them to the point when they lost not only their heads but also their hearts.

It might perhaps have been the lazy indifference with which he regarded them, which was very different from the alert commands that he gave when dealing with his men.

'You treat me as if I were a doll or a puppet – just a plaything that has no other function in life except to amuse you,' one charmer had said petulantly.

It was a statement that was echoed in various ways by almost every woman who had preceded or followed her.

The truth lay in the fact that the Earl did not take women seriously.

With his soldiers it was different.

The men he commanded adored him because to him they were always individuals, and although he expected implicit obedience he was never too busy to listen to a man's grievances or his personal difficulties.

24

It was not conceit which had the Earl bolt his door against the lovely women who would have been only too thrilled to sit at his bedside and hold his hand after Mr Newell had operated on him.

Nor was it frustration at being unable to make love to them physically.

It was in truth that he found women bores unless he was actively pursuing them, indulging in the cut and thrust of a flirtation which inevitably ended in bed.

So, of his own free will, the Earl had confined himself to the conversation of Batley and the interchange of pleasantries that took place every day between himself and Colonel Berkeley's Comptroller of the Household, Mr Knightley.

Now, unexpectedly, entirely by chance, a woman had brought him a new interest, and if she had planned it Giselda could not have aroused him more effectively than by being elusive, secretive and mysterious.

The Earl was used to women who told him about themselves long before he asked them to do so and who were only too willing to talk interminably to him so long as they were the subject of the conversation.

It was not only pity that he felt for Giselda because she was so undernourished; it was also that she positively interested him as a person.

How could it be possible that a girl who was obviously a lady, well educated and of a refinement which showed that she had come from a good home, should have been brought to the point of starvation?

Not only herself, but also her mother and her young brother.

How could they suddenly have been reduced to poverty? How if her father's death had brought a financial crisis, had there been no relations, no one they could turn to to give them at least a roof over their heads?

The Earl did not sleep as Giselda had suggested he

should. Instead he lay thinking about her and wondering how he could persuade her to talk about herself.

'I dare say when I learn the story it will be a very ordinary one,' he thought. 'Cards, drink, other women! What else is there that ensures that when a man dies, his family is left without support?'

Although he laughed at himself for being interested, there was no doubt that he was intrigued and insatiably curious and the afternoon seemed to pass remarkably slowly.

He had just begun to wonder if in fact Giselda had other reasons for not returning, when the door opened and she came in.

She had changed her gown, he noticed at once, for one that was more attractive; at the same time it was definitely dated as the other had been.

She carried a shawl over one arm and on the other a basket.

The plain bonnet which framed her thin face was trimmed with blue ribbons which matched the colour of her eyes, and the Earl thought perhaps for the first time that she would be beautiful if she was not so thin.

'I am sorry, My Lord, to have been so long,' she said, 'but I had to buy the ingredients my mother required for the ointment and it took a little time to make. However, I have it with me now, and I am sure you will be much more comfortable once I have applied it.'

'I was wondering why you were so long.'

'May I do your leg now?' Giselda asked. 'Then perhaps, if you do not want me any more, I could go home.'

'I expect you to dine with me.'

Giselda was still for a moment, then she said quietly:

'Is that really necessary? You gave me luncheon and I was grateful. I guessed, before they told me downstairs that you do not usually eat so much at midday, that you were being kind.'

Although she spoke gratefully the Earl had the impression that she half-resented his generosity simply because it offended her pride.

'Hungry or not,' he said, 'you will dine with me. I am tired of eating alone.'

'May I point out that Your Lordship has many friends who are far more suitable as dinner-companions than I am?'

'Are you arguing with me again?' the Earl asked.

'I am afraid so. I thought that Your Lordship would not require my services so late.'

'You have another engagement – some *Beau* who is waiting for you?'

'It is nothing like that.'

'Are you expecting me to believe that you are anxious to leave merely because you wish to return to your mother and your brother?'

There was silence for a moment and as Giselda did not reply the Earl said sharply :

'I asked you a question and I expect an answer.'

'I think Your Lordship will understand when I say that you have engaged me to attend to your leg and to wait on you,' Giselda said after a moment. 'I am still a servant, My Lord.'

'And as a servant you must learn to do as you are told,' the Earl said. 'If I am eccentric or peculiar, if you like, in wishing the company of one of my servants at dinner, I see no reason why they should not comply with what is not a request but an order.'

'Yes, My Lord. But you must admit that it is unusual.'

'And how do you know it is unusual for me?' the Earl replied. 'I know nothing about you, Giselda, you know nothing about me. We met today for the first time. Doubtless you had not heard of me until yesterday.'

'Of course I . . '

Giselda stopped suddenly.

The Earl looked at her sharply.

'Finish that sentence!'

There was no reply.

'You were going to say of course you had heard of me. How could you have done that?'

Again there was silence. Then as if the words were dragged from her lips Giselda said:

'You are .. famous. I think everyone has heard of you .. just as they have heard of the .. Duke of Wellington.'

It was not entirely a truthful answer, the Earl was well aware of that, but he did not press the point.

'Very well, I concede that I am famous, but is that any reason why you should refuse to dine with me?'

Giselda put the basket down on the table.

'What I am trying to say, My Lord, is that as your servant it would be a mistake for me to assume any different position.'

'Am I offering you one?'

'No .. My Lord, not exactly .. but .. '

'Let me make this quite clear,' the Earl said. 'I do not intend to be tied by convention, rules or regulations that may apply in some households, but certainly not in this. If I decide to have one of the scullions to dinner, I see no reason why he should not come upstairs although he would doubtless dislike it as much as I should.'

His eyes were on Giselda's face and he went on:

'But where you are concerned, you have a very different status. You are here to minister to me, whether it means to bandage my leg or to give me your company at the rather awkward meals which I am obliged to take from my bedside.'

His voice was hard and authoritative as he continued:

'It is up to me and not to anyone else – I make the choice – I choose what I wish to do, and I see no reason why anyone in my employment, man or woman, should oppose me on such an insignificant matter.'

The Earl spoke in a manner which those who had served under him knew only too well, and Giselda capitulated exactly as they would have done.

She curtsied.

'Very good, My Lord. If you will permit me to remove my bonnet and to fetch some hot water, I will now attend to your leg.'

'The sooner the better!' the Earl said loftily.

Giselda left the room, and when he was alone he chuckled to himself.

He knew that he had found the way to treat her, a way in which she found it hard to oppose him. He told himself with some satisfaction that, if he had not won a battle, at least he had been the victor in a small skirmish.

Giselda came back with the hot water.

Once again there was a little pain when the bandages were removed, but her hands were very gentle and the Earl noted with approval that she was not in the least embarrassed in tending him as a man.

There were no women nurses obtainable; in fact nursing was considered a job essentially for men.

But the Earl had thought when he was on active service that the wounded who were attended to in Convents were more fortunate than those who were at the mercy of rough Orderlies in the overcrowded hospitals.

'How have you gained so much experience?' he asked.

As he spoke he was aware it was a probing question which doubtless Giselda would try to avoid.

'I have had a lot of bandaging to do,' she answered.

'For your family?'

She did not answer but merely pulled the sheet over his leg. Then she tidied the bed and patted up his pillows.

'I am waiting for an answer, Giselda,' the Earl said.

She gave him a smile which had something mischievous in it.

'I think, My Lord, we should talk of more interesting things. Are you aware that the Duke of Wellington is coming to open the new Assembly Rooms?'

'The Duke?' the Earl exclaimed. 'Who told you this?'

'It is all over the town. He has been here before, of

course, but not since Waterloo. The town is to be illuminated in his honour, and there is to be a triumphal arch of welcome across the High Street.'

'I have seen arches before,' the Earl remarked, 'but I would like to see the Duke.'

'He will be staying in Colonel Riddell's house which is not far from here.'

'Then he will undoubtedly call and see me,' the Earl said, 'and I expect you would like to meet the great hero of Waterloo.'

Giselda turned away.

'No,' she said. 'No .. I have no desire to .. meet the Duke.'

The Earl looked at her in surprise.

'No desire to meet the Duke?' he repeated. 'I always believed that every woman in England was on her knees night after night praying that by some lucky chance she would encounter the hero of her dreams! Why are you the exception?'

Again there was silence.

'Surely you can give a simple answer to a simple question?' the Earl asked in a tone of exasperation. 'I asked you, Giselda, why you do not wish to meet the Duke?'

'Shall I say that I have my .. reasons?' Giselda answered.

'A more damned silly answer I have never heard,' the Earl stormed. 'Let me tell you, Giselda, that it is very bad for my health to be treated as though I were a half-witted child who could not stand the truth. What is the truth?'

'I think, My Lord, that as your dinner will be arriving in a few minutes I would like to go to my own room and wash my hands after attending to your leg.'

Before the Earl could reply Giselda had gone from the room.

He stared after her for a moment in exasperation, then in amusement.

'Now what has she got to be so mysterious about?' he asked aloud.

Then as the door opened and his valet came in he said:

'Have you any news for me, Batley?'

'I am afraid, My Lord, I have drawn a blank. I had a chat, as one might say, with the Housekeeper. But she knows nothing; as she told Your Lordship, she took the young lady on without a reference.'

It did not escape the Earl's notice that Batley, who was an acute judge of people, referred to Giselda as a lady.

He was well aware of the difference in Batley's tone when he spoke of someone as being a 'person' or a 'young woman'.

It only confirmed what he knew himself. At the same time it was interesting, and he knew too that Batley had got over his pique at Giselda taking over what had previously been one of his duties.

Normally he would have been jealous of another servant valeting his master or in any way intruding on the somewhat unique relationship between them. But apparently Giselda had stepped in without opposition and that to the Earl was significant.

'You must go on trying, Batley,' he said aloud. 'It is unusual for you and me not to be able to find out what we want to know. You remember how useful you were in Portugal when you found out where the merchants had hidden their wines?'

'That was very much easier, M'Lord,' Batley said. 'Women are women all the world over and the Portuguese are as susceptible as any other nationality.'

'I will take your word for it,' the Earl said.

He was conscious of a twinkle in the eyes of his valet as they both remembered a very delectable little *Señorita* with whom he had spent several pleasant nights when they passed through Lisbon.

There was very little in the Earl's life that Batley did not know about. He was devoted and he had for his mas-

31

ter a respect and admiration that amounted almost to adoration.

At the same time he retained his individuality and his own independence of thought and judgement.

Batley was shrewd and the Earl knew that he could always rely on him to pass judgement on a man or a woman which would not be far from the truth.

'Tell me exactly what you think of our new acquisition to the household, Batley,' he asked now.

'If you are speaking of Miss Chart, M'Lord,' Batley replied, 'she's a lady, I'd bet my shirt on that. But there's something she's hiding, M'Lord, and it's worrying her, although I can't quite understand why.'

'And that, Batley, is what we have to find out,' the Earl replied.

He thought as he spoke that, however reluctant Giselda might be to dine with him, he was looking forward to it.

2

'Where are you going?'

Giselda with one arm full of books turned from the desk from which she had taken a number of letters.

'I am going to the Post Office first, My Lord,' she replied, 'to try to persuade that lazy Postmaster that your letters are urgent. Everyone in the town is complaining about him because he is so dilatory about despatching the mail. I am not certain whether I should speak to him coaxingly or severely.'

The Earl smiled.

'I should imagine in your case coaxingly might be more effective.'

'One can never be sure with that sort of man,' Giselda said.

'And you are taking the books back to the Library?' the Earl asked glancing at the pile in her arm.

'I will try to find something which will amuse you,' she replied in a worried tone, 'but Your Lordship is very critical, and although Williams' Library is the best in the County, I can find little to please you.'

The Earl did not reply because, to tell the truth, he enjoyed criticising the literature that Giselda read to him aloud for the simple reason that he liked to hear her opinion on the various subjects they discussed.

He was astonished to find that so young a woman not only had a very decided point of view on most matters including politics, but also could substantiate her opinions from other books she had read on the subject.

At times they argued quite violently, and when he was

alone at night the Earl would go over in his mind what had been said and find surprisingly that Giselda was often better informed on some matters than he was himself.

She was wearing her bonnet with the blue ribbons, and as there was a wind despite the warmth of the day she wore a light blue shawl over her gown.

Looking at her the Earl decided that in the week she had been in his employment, eating two good meals a day in his company, she was already less thin and there was a touch of colour in her cheeks which had not been there before.

At the same time, he thought, they had a long way to go before she reached what should be her normal weight, even though she assured him that she had always been slender.

The difficulty, he found, was to persuade Giselda to accept anything from him except her wages.

He had thought on the second day of her entering his employment that he would be clever and order such large meals that what she took home would be more than enough for her family and herself.

But he had come up against what he told her was her 'damnable pride'.

As they finished luncheon he noted with satisfaction that there was a whole chicken untouched besides a plump pigeon and a number of other dishes which were perfectly conveyable.

'You had better pack up what is left,' he said casually.

Giselda had looked at the chicken and said:

'I cannot do that, My Lord.'

'Why not?' he enquired sharply.

'Because I suspect that Your Lordship ordered more food than was necessary, and what is left over, being untouched, can be used again.'

'Are you telling me that you will not accept this food, which you well know your family needs?' the Earl enquired.

'We may be poor, My Lord, but we have our pride.'

'The poor cannot afford pride,' the Earl said scathingly.

'And when they get to that stage,' Giselda retorted, 'it means that they have lost their character and personality and are little more than animals.'

She paused to say defiantly :

'I am grateful for your thought of me, My Lord, but I will not accept your charity.'

The Earl made a sound of impatience, then reaching forward he pulled off one leg of the chicken with his bare hands.

'Now it is acceptable?' he asked.

There was a pause before Giselda said :

'Because I know the Chef will either throw it away or feed it to the dog I will take it, My Lord, but another time I will refuse to do so.'

'You are the most foolish, idiotic, tiresome woman I have ever met in my whole life!' the Earl stormed.

She had not answered, but had merely packed up the chicken leaving the pigeon on its plate.

The Earl learnt in the succeeding days that Giselda had to be handled with care, otherwise her pride created obstacles which even he could not scale.

What was more exasperating was that despite every effort on his part he still knew no more about her than he had the first day he had engaged her services.

One thing however was very clear.

Under her ministrations his leg was healing better and quicker than Mr Newell, the Surgeon, had dared to hope.

'You must rest while I am away,' Giselda said now, 'and please do not get out of bed as you tried to do yesterday. You know what Mr Newell said.'

'I refuse to be mollycoddled by you and these damned doctors,' the Earl growled.

At the same time he knew that what the Surgeon had said was common-sense.

'Your leg, My Lord, is far better than I had anticipated,'

he answered after he had examined it. 'But Your Lordship will appreciate that to get away the grapeshot I had to probe very deeply.'

'I have not forgotten that!' the Earl said grimly.

'I will be frank,' the Surgeon went on, 'and tell you now that I thought when I found so much had been left behind and how badly it was festering, that you might still have to lose your leg. But miracles still happen, and in your case this is undoubtedly true.'

'I am grateful,' the Earl managed to say as the Surgeon's fingers moved over the scars to find them clean and healing, as he had put it, 'from beneath'.

'How soon can I get out of bed?' the Earl asked.

'Not for at least another week, My Lord. As you well know, any sharp movement or even the weight of your body might start the wounds bleeding afresh. It only requires a little patience.'

'A virtue, unfortunately, I have never possessed,' the Earl remarked.

'Then, My Lord, it is something you must learn now,' Thomas Newell had replied.

He then commended Giselda on her bandaging.

'If you are ever in need of employment, Miss Chart, I have a hundred patients waiting for you.'

'You sound busy,' the Earl remarked.

'I have a waiting-list from here to next week,' Thomas Newell said not without a touch of pride in his voice, 'and they are not only veterans of the war, like yourself, My Lord, but members of the nobility who come here from as far away as Scotland, and even from across the Channel. Sometimes I wonder how I can possibly accommodate them all.'

'There is a penalty attaching to everything,' the Earl smiled, 'even to a famous reputation.'

'That is something Your Lordship must have discovered yourself,' Thomas Newell said courteously before he took his leave.

'If you move about,' Giselda said now, 'you will disturb the bandages, and if you do that I shall be very angry.'

She paused as if she had remembered something.

'My mother is making some more ointment. Perhaps I had better call for it on my way back.'

'I owe you for the last lot your mother made,' the Earl said. 'How much did it come to?'

'A shilling and threepence-halfpenny,' Giselda answered.

'I presume you expect me to give you the halfpenny, or would you accept a fourpenny piece?'

'I can give you change,' Giselda said with a twinkle in here eye.

She was well aware that he was teasing her, half playfully and half seriously, because she refused to accept any money except what he actually owed her.

'You infuriate me,' he said as she turned towards the door.

'Then that will give your Lordship something to think about while I am gone,' she answered. 'Batley is listening for your bell if you should wish for anything.'

With that she was gone and the Earl lay back against his pillows to wonder for the thousandth time who she was and why she would not tell him about herself.

He had never imagined that any woman who was so young — Giselda had admitted to being nineteen — could have so much self-assurance when it came to dealing with him. Yet he knew that in other ways she was in fact very sensitive and shy.

There was some quality about her that he had never found in any other woman, and what he admired better than anything else was her air of serenity.

When he was not talking to her she would sit quietly reading in a corner of the room and make no effort to thrust herself into prominence or attract his attention.

It was a new experience for the Earl to be with a woman who not only made no effort to flirt with him, but seemed in fact perfectly content to be anonymous except when he required her services.

He was used to being with women who used every wile in the female repertoire to focus his attention upon themselves. Who looked at him with an invitation in their eyes, and challenged him with a provocative twist to their lips.

Giselda was as natural in her behaviour as if he were her brother or — sobering thought — her father, and she talked to him frankly on every subject except herself.

'I will find out what is behind all this if it is the last thing I do,' the Earl vowed.

At that moment the door opened and a man put his head round it.

'Are you awake?' a deep voice said.

The Earl turned to look at the intruder.

'Fitz!' he exclaimed. 'Come in! I am delighted to see you!'

'I hoped you would be,' Colonel Berkeley said entering the room.

He seemed with his height and his broad shoulders almost overpowering to the Earl who must regard him from the bed.

'Dammit, Fitz!' he exclaimed. 'You look disgustingly and outrageously healthy! How are your horses?'

'Waiting for you to ride them,' Colonel Berkeley replied. 'I now have sixty top-notchers, Talbot, which I intend to put at the disposal of anyone who wishes to hunt them this season, and you can have first pick.'

'It certainly is an inducement to get well quickly,' the Earl said.

'You are better?'

'Very much better. Newell is a good man.'

'I told you he was.'

'You were absolutely right, and I am extremely thankful that I took your advice and came to Cheltenham.'

'That is what I wanted you to say,' Colonel Berkeley smiled. 'As I have told you before, this town is unique!'

There was a pride in his voice that was unmistakable and the Earl laughed.

'How soon are you going to re-christen it "Berkeleyville"? That is what it ought to be named.'

'I have thought of it,' Colonel Berkeley replied, 'but since Cheltenham is of Saxon origin it might be a mistake to change it.'

'Why are you here? I thought it was impossible for you to leave the Castle.'

'I have called a meeting to plan the Duke of Wellington's reception. You have heard that he is coming here?'

'Yes, I have been told so. It is true?'

'Of course it is true! Where else would the "Iron Duke's" physicians send him but to Cheltenham?'

'Where indeed?' the Earl asked mockingly.

'He is staying with Riddell at Cambray Cottage, which is to be re-christened "Wellington Mansion", and naturally I shall ask him to open the new Assembly Rooms, plant an oak tree and attend the theatre.'

'In fact a riot of fun and gaiety!' the Earl said cynically.

'Good God, I cannot suggest much else,' Colonel Berkeley replied. 'He is bringing his Duchess with him!'

'So everyone will have to be on their best behaviour.'

'Of course, except for me. You have never known me to be anything but outrageous.'

'That is true,' the Earl said, 'and what, Fitz, are you up to now?'

'I have found the most fascinating woman,' Colonel Berkeley said seating himself on the side of the bed, the brilliant polish on his hessian boots reflecting the sunshine coming in through the windows.

'Another? Who is she?'

'Her name is Maria Foote,' Colonel Berkeley replied. 'She is an actress and I met her last year when I performed at the theatre in her Benefit.'

'What happened outside the theatre?' the Earl asked.

'She was for a short time somewhat elusive,' Colonel Berkeley replied.

'But now . . ?'

'I have set her up in one of my other cottages.'

The Earl laughed.

'How many more have you got, Fitz?'

'Quite a number,' Colonel Berkeley replied, 'but Maria and I are extremely happy. She is beautiful, Talbot, really beautiful, and you must meet her as soon as you are well enough.'

'Then you are not staying here?' the Earl enquired.

'No. I shall be with Maria tonight, and I must return to the Castle tomorrow, but I shall be back at the end of the week. You are not bored?'

'No, I am not bored,' the Earl said truthfully, 'and Newell hopes that I shall be up in a week or so.'

'You must come to the opening of the Assembly Rooms,' Colonel Berkeley said.

He did not miss the grimace that the Earl made and laughed.

'I will let you off if you will come and see me act at the theatre with my own cast in a new piece which I know you will find amusing. It has been written by a young man of whom I have great hopes.'

The Earl was well aware that amongst his many other activities Colonel Berkeley enjoyed acting.

He had his own company of amateur performers, and every month or so they performed at the Theatre Royal, to an audience who came not only to enjoy the play, but also to gaze awe-struck at the Colonel himself whose wild and profligate behaviour fascinated them.

The Colonel however found that Amateur theatricals did not satisfy him and he would act his favourite parts with players of the standing of John Kemble and Mrs Siddons.

The fees he offered were large and he could guarantee

that the audience would include a host of his distinguished friends.

Actors were looked down on as being a feckless, immoral crowd and the Colonel's association with them still further damaged his reputation.

'I shall be delighted to come and applaud,' the Earl replied. 'What is this masterpiece called?'

'It is entitled *The Villain Unmasked*,' Colonel Berkeley replied. 'Is that dramatic enough for you?'

'And you are the hero?'

'No, of course not! I am the villain. What other part would I play when the plot concerns the ravishing of a young and beautiful girl?'

The Earl threw back his head and laughed.

'Fitz! You are incorrigible! As if people do not talk enough about you as it is already.'

'I like them talking,' Colonel Berkeley said. 'It brings them to Cheltenham, it makes them spend their money, and it justifies my contention that the town is far too small; we must build new houses, larger public buildings and lay out more avenues.'

Building was the Colonel's pet hobby-horse and he talked about it for some time, telling the Earl of his plans to make Cheltenham 'The Queen of Watering Places'.

'Have you heard the latest jingle about the town?' he asked.

'Which one?'

Rising to his feet the Colonel recited with fervour:

> '*Men of every class and order,*
> *All the genera and species,*
> *Dukes with aides-de-camp in leashes,*
> *Marquesses in tandem traces,*
> *Lords in couples, Counts in pairs,*
> *Coveys of their spendthrift heirs . . .*'

'Very appropriate!' the Earl said dryly.

'There is a lot more but I will not bore you with it,' the Colonel said, 'except that one line ends with "flocks of charmers"! That's true!'

Inevitably, the Earl thought, the Colonel's conversation got back to women, and after expounding somewhat crudely on 'the charmers' in the town, he said:

'I saw a rather attractive girl leaving here just as I arrived. I asked the Butler who she was and he informed me that she was your nurse.'

The Earl did not reply and the Colonel said with undisguised interest:

'Come on, Talbot, you old fox! Since when have you required a female nurse? Or is that only a polite name for it?'

'It happens to be the truth,' the Earl said. 'Batley means well, but he is heavy-handed and quite by chance I found Giselda had some experience of bandaging. Even Newell congratulated her.'

'And what else is she good at?' Colonel Berkeley asked, an innuendo in the words.

The Earl shook his head.

'Nothing like that. She is a lady, although I understand that her family has fallen on hard times.'

'I thought she looked attractive, although I only had a quick glimpse of her,' the Colonel said reflectively.

'Hands off, Fitz!' the Earl said firmly.

'Of course – if she is your property,' Colonel Berkeley said. 'But I am surprised. I remember your lecturing me once and saying you did not amuse yourself with your own servants or anyone else's.'

'That is still true,' the Earl answered, 'and I certainly would not allow you to amuse yourself with mine!'

'Is that a challenge?' Colonel Berkeley enquired with a sudden glint in his eyes.

'Try it and I will knock your head off,' the Earl retorted. 'I may be a cripple at the moment, but you know as well as I do, Fitz, that we are pretty well matched when it comes to fisticuffs and once I am fit again . . . '

He paused, then laughed.

'We are being far too damned serious over this, but leave Giselda alone. She has never met anyone like you and I do not want her spoilt.'

He was well aware that the Colonel found it impossible to resist a pretty face wherever he found it.

At the same time because they were such old friends he knew, or at least he thought he knew, that Giselda would be safe as long as she was under his care.

But Colonel Berkeley's way with women was too notorious not to leave the Earl with a feeling of unease.

He had in fact until this moment not thought of Giselda as being desirable or indeed in the category of a woman who must be pursued, as sportsmen like the Colonel pursued a fox.

But now he realised that she had a grace which made her figure, thin though it was, an undeniable enticement, and that her big eyes filling her small, pale face were beautiful rather differently from the way he had interpreted beauty in the past.

All his women had been, he thought, like full-blown roses, big-breasted, seductive, voluptuous, and in contrast Giselda was the exact opposite.

It was perhaps her reserve which had made him not consider her as a woman to be seduced and conquered until Colonel Berkeley had put the idea into his mind.

And yet now the Earl found himself thinking of her in a very different way from how he had thought of her before.

For the first time he wondered if it was right that she should walk through the town by herself without an attendant of some sort.

Behaviour was far more free and easy in Cheltenham than in London but, even so, he had the idea that a girl of Giselda's age, if she was shopping or attending the Spa to drink the waters, should be accompanied if not by a Chaperon, at least by an abigail or a footman.

Then he told himself he was being ridiculous.

Giselda, whatever her antecedents about which he still was in ignorance, was still a servant. He paid her as he paid Batley, and the hundreds of servants that he employed at Lynd Park, his country seat in Oxfordshire.

He wondered whether, when he was well enough to return home, Giselda would go with him, and was almost sure without asking her that she would refuse.

Once again he found it frustrating to realise how little he knew of her.

How could her family be so poor? And why did she never talk about her mother or her small brother?

'It is unnatural,' the Earl thought savagely, and once again was determined to force the information from her lips.

Giselda returned an hour later and the Earl, despite his resolution to do nothing of the sort, had been watching the clock.

'You have been a hell of a time,' he growled as she came into the bedroom.

'The shops are crowded,' she said, 'especially Williams' Library.'

She gave a little laugh.

'I wish you could have seen the people all queueing to get on the weighing-machine.'

'The weighing-machine?' the Earl queried.

'Yes, all the celebrities and in fact everyone who comes to Cheltenham try out the weighing-machine. Those who are fat hope that the waters will make them slim, and those who are thin are convinced that they will put on weight.'

'Did you weigh yourself?' the Earl enquired.

'I would not waste my penny on such nonsense!'

'I am sure you would find that your weight is very different from what it was a week ago.'

Giselda smiled.

'I admit to having to let out the waist of my gowns at least an inch,' she answered, 'but I know, because you continually say so, that you think I am just a bag of bones and you hate thin women.'

'She may be thin,' the Earl thought looking at her critically, 'but her figure is exquisite, like that of a young goddess.'

Then he told himself he was being a poetic fool.

It was only Fitz Berkeley who had put such ideas into his head, and he had been right in saying that the Earl had never concerned himself from an amatory point of view with a servant, and he did not intend to do so now.

'Here are your books,' Giselda was saying, setting them down beside him. 'I am sure they will please you, at least I hope so, and quite frankly I chose those I want to read myself.'

'For which, I suppose, I should be grateful.'

'I can always change them.'

She turned towards the door.

'Where are you going.' the Earl asked.

'To take off my bonnet and wash my hands. When I come back I will read you the newspaper if Your Lordship is too lazy to read it for yourself!'

'You will do what I tell you to do,' the Earl said sharply.

But the door had shut behind her and he was not certain if she had heard his last remark.

·   ·   ·   ·   ·

The following day Giselda was late in arriving, which in itself was unusual. What was more, as soon as she appeared, the Earl was aware that something untoward had occurred.

He was used now to her smile first thing in the morning, to the lilt of her voice and the manner in which without being impertinent she would answer him back and could usually tease him into a good humour.

45

But this morning she was very pale and there was a darkness in her eyes which the Earl knew meant she was worried.

She dressed his leg in silence, and when she had finished, she tidied the pillows and took the discarded bandages from the room.

The Earl was shaved and washed by Batley before Giselda arrived.

Batley also made the bed either with the Housekeeper or one of the housemaids, so that when Giselda came back to the Earl no one was likely to intrude and she was alone with him.

Because he had grown used to watching the expressions on her face and had become unusually perceptive where she was concerned, he was aware that she had something to say to him but was wise enough not to ask questions.

He merely watched her as she moved restlessly about the room, tidying things which had already been tidied, patting up the cushions in one of the armchairs and re-arranging the vase of roses which stood on a side table.

Finally she came towards the bed and the Earl knew that she had made up her mind to speak.

He thought that because something was upsetting her, her cheek-bones once again seemed very prominent, and had the idea that her hands were trembling a little as she drew nearer to him.

'I want .. to ask you .. something,' she said in a low voice.

'What is it?' he enquired.

'I do not .. know how to put it into .. words.'

'I can be understanding if necessary.'

'I know that,' she answered. 'Batley has told me how everyone in your Regiment came to you with their .. problems, and how you always .. solved them.'

'Then let me solve yours.'

'Y . you may .. think it very .. strange.'

46

'I cannot answer that until you tell me what it is,' the Earl said.

She stood silent by his bedside, and now he could sense the agitation within her so that with difficulty he forced himself to wait.

Finally she said in a very low voice:

'I have .. heard, and I do not think I am mistaken, that there are .. g . gentlemen who will pay large sums of money for a girl who is .. p . pure. I want .. I must have .. £50 immediately .. and I thought perhaps you could find me .. someone to give me .. that .. amount.'

The Earl was stunned into silence.

Then as Giselda did not look at him and her eyelashes were dark against her pale cheeks he exclaimed:

'Good God! Do you know what you are saying? And if you want £50 ..'

Just for a moment she looked at him, then she turned sharply on her heel and walked towards the door.

'Where are you going?'

'I ∴ th . thought you would .. understand ..'

She had almost left the room as the Earl roared:

'Come here! Do you hear me? Come here immediately!'

He thought she was about to refuse him. Then as if the command in his voice compelled her she very slowly closed the door again and came towards the bed.

'Let me understand this quite clearly,' the Earl said. 'You want £50 but you will not accept it from me?'

'You know I will not take money .. unless I can give something in .. return,' Giselda said fiercely.

The Earl was about to argue, then he knew it would be useless.

He was well aware that Giselda's pride was so much a part of her whole character that if he persisted in thrusting his money upon her she was quite likely to walk out of his life and he would never see her again.

Diplomatically he played for time.

'Forgive me, Giselda, you took me by surprise. I understand your feelings in this matter, but have you really
considered what you are suggesting?'

'I have .. considered it,' Giselda said, 'and it is the only
.. solution I can find. I thought perhaps it would be easy
for you to find .. someone who would .. pay for what I
can .. offer him.'

'It is of course possible,' the Earl said slowly.

'Then you will do it?'

'That depends,' he replied. 'I think I would not be asking too much, Giselda, if I enquire why you need such a
large sum so urgently.'

She turned from the bedside to walk across the room to
the window.

She stood looking out and the Earl knew she was debat-
ing with herself as to whether she should trust him with
her secret, or whether she should refuse.

Finally because he knew she felt he was her only
hope of getting the money she required, she said in a low
voice:

'My brother .. if he is ever to walk again .. must be
operated on by Mr Newell.'

'Your brother has been injured?'

'He was knocked down two months ago by a Phaeton
that was travelling too fast. He was trampled on by the
horses .. and a .. wheel passed over him.'

The last words were spoken almost as if the horror of
what had occurred was still too poignant to be expressed
in words.

'So that was why you came to Cheltenham!'

'Yes.'

'And you have been waiting for your brother to see
Newell?'

'Yes.'

'Why did you not tell me?'

She did not reply and he knew what the answer was.

She and her family would not accept charity.

'It must be a very serious operation if Newell is charging so much,' the Earl said after a moment.

'It is, but he will also keep Rupert in his private hospital for a few days and that is included in the £50.'

'You have no other way of getting the money?'

It was an unnecessary question, the Earl knew. They would not be starving now if they had had any resources.

Giselda turned from the window.

'Will you . . help me?'

'I will help you,' the Earl replied, 'but perhaps not in the way you suggest.'

'I must . . earn the money.'

'I am aware of that.'

She came nearer to him and now he thought the expression in her eyes was one of trust.

Experienced though he was in the problems of other people, the Earl thought that he had never in his life had such an extraordinary request or one that he found so incredible.

And yet he realised that where Giselda was concerned there was little alternative.

It was true, and she was not misinformed, there were men who would pay large sums, although not often as much as £50, to the keepers of expensive Brothels who would provide them with untouched virgins.

The Earl was well aware, as were all his contemporaries, that the Temple of Flora in St James' catered for every type of vice, and there were other places whose Proprietors haunted the parks in search of pretty nurse-maids from the country and met the Stage coaches when they arrived with rosy-cheeked girls looking for domestic employment.

That Giselda should suggest such a thing was to the Earl as surprising and sensational as if a cannonball had been fired in the quiet bedroom.

He realised she was waiting and after a moment he said:

'Will you give me a few hours to think this over, Giselda? I suppose, while I am considering the matter and we are finding a solution, you would not allow me to lend you the money?'

'Mr Newell said he can perform the operation on Thursday.'

'That gives us two days.'

'Yes . . two days.'

'I would like longer.'

'I . . cannot . . wait.'

He knew she had refused his suggestion without actually saying so and he wondered whether if he raged at her it would make any difference. Then he knew that nothing he could say would make her take money from him.

Because the tension between them was so strong, again the Earl played for time.

'Suppose you read me the news?' he suggested. 'I want to hear what is happening in the world outside. It will also give me a chance, Giselda, to adjust myself to this quite astounding request.'

She made a helpless little gesture with her hands as if she explained without words that she had no alternative.

Then obediently she picked up the *Cheltenham Chronicle* and seating herself on a chair at the bedside she started to read in her soft voice first the headlines, then the leading article.

That was the order in which the Earl liked things done, but this morning he did not hear one word of what Giselda read.

He was turning over and over in his mind every possible way by which he could prevent her from sacrificing herself to save her brother.

From the conversations he had had with Giselda the Earl was certain she was very innocent.

They had not actually discussed the intimacy between a man and a woman, but from things she had said he thought that, like most girls of her age, she had little if any idea of what happened when two people made love together.

Because she was so sensitive, so innocent and, above all, well-bred, the Earl knew that anything that occurred in the circumstances she had suggested would be a shock and perhaps a terror beyond anything she had ever dreamt of or imagined.

He realised too that because he was an invalid and because she was so innocent, it had never for one moment struck her that he might in fact offer her the money on his own behalf.

He had been right, he thought, in thinking that she did not look on him as a man who might desire her as a woman.

In fact never in their relationship had she ever at any time been self-conscious about tending to his wounds, arranging his pillows or being in close proximity to him.

His own attitude had, the Earl realised, contributed to this by the fact that he either ordered her about or discussed things that interested them both in the same manner as he would have disscued them with a man.

Now he knew that it would be impossible for him to stand aside and let Giselda prostitute herself, as she wished to do. But the difficulty was how to prevent it.

He was still not well enough to play the lover, even if he wished to do so, and even to suggest such a thing would be to change the relationship between them in a manner which the Earl felt would be extremely regrettable.

At the moment she trusted him. She had come to him in her difficulty and with her problems, and that at least made things easier than they might have been.

But he knew only too well how fiercely she would resist any attempt on his part to give her money.

What is more she would not be deceived into believing

that he desired her as a woman, when up to this moment there had never been the slightest indication of it in his manner towards her.

'What the devil can I do?' the Earl asked himself.

When finally Giselda set down the paper he still had no solution of any sort to offer.

She looked at him enquiringly, and he was wondering what on earth he could say to her when Batley came into the room.

'Excuse me, M'Lord, but Captain Henry Somercote has called and wishes to see Your Lordship.'

The interruption was, the Earl thought, for the moment a Godsend.

'I shall be delighted as well you know, Batley, to see Captain Somercote. Ask him to come up.'

Giselda rose to her feet.

'We will talk about this a little later,' the Earl said.

'Thank you, My Lord.'

She curtsied and as she went from the room the Earl thought that the suffering on her face was even more marked than when she had merely looked starved.

'I have to find a way out of this problem,' he told himself frantically.

Captain Somercote came into the room looking a Tulip of Fashion with a starched cravat which was almost dazzling in its whiteness, the points of his collar high above his sunburnt chin.

'Henry!' the Earl exclaimed. 'I am delighted to see you! What on earth has brought you to Cheltenham?'

'I thought you might have expected me,' Henry Somercote replied.

He was a good-looking young man, a few years younger than the Earl. They had served in the same Regiment and fought side by side at Waterloo.

They were also related, although the connection was slight, and they had in fact known each other since they were children.

'I am here to scatter rosebuds in the path of the con-
quering hero,' Henry Somercote said seating himself in a
comfortable chair.

'Of course I might have guessed that where the Duke
was you would be also.'

'Am I ever off duty?' Captain Somercote asked, who
had been an *Aide-de-Camp* to Wellington at Waterloo.
'His Grace has now almost adopted me and he bamboozles
the C.O. into sending me ahead of him whenever he has to
make a public appearance.'

'I should imagine that is no hardship.'

'Good Lord, no! I much prefer it to "square-bashing",
but I do not mind telling you, I find myself in some jolly
queer places.'

'Well, I for one am delighted that you have come to
Cheltenham,' the Earl said.

'The first thing I thought of when the Duke told me
where he was going was that I should see you,' Captain
Somercote said. 'Are you better?'

'Much better!' the Earl said firmly.

'That is a relief. When you left Belgium I thought you
were for the "high-jump" and all because you would not
let the old Sawbones take your leg off.'

'How right I was,' the Earl remarked. 'It is now well on
the way to recovery, but I have to thank the Surgeon here
for that.'

'I must say you look better,' Captain Somercote said
regarding the Earl critically, 'but you will put on weight
if you lie in bed for too long.'

'That is what I keep thinking myself,' the Earl answered, 'but I am bullied most effectively into staying
where I am until the wounds have healed.'

'Well, I do not suppose you lack for entertainment in
this house,' Henry Somercote said. 'How is the Colonel? I
found the whole town was talking of him as soon as I
arrived, but that is nothing unusual.'

'Fitz was here this morning as it happens,' the Earl replied. 'He has taken a new beauty under his protection – Maria Foote.'

'I have seen her. She is beautiful,' Henry Somercote remarked. 'Trust the Colonel to get there first! I would not mind having a go at her myself!'

'I would not advise you to interfere now that they are firmly established,' the Earl said. 'Fitz has a way of resenting any encroachment on his preserves, and he is very handy with a pistol.'

'I am not such a fool as that,' Henry Somercote replied. 'Besides, the town is full of pretty women. There is plenty of choice.'

He smiled, then said:

'Do you want to hear the bad news?'

'You would not be able to keep yourself from telling me sooner or later,' the Earl replied, 'so I had better hear it sooner.'

'It is about Julius.'

'It would be!' the Earl groaned. 'What has he been up to now?'

'Making more of a fool of himself than usual.'

'Damn the young idiot!' the Earl exclaimed. 'I suppose he is in debt again! I told him the last time I paid up that was the end and by God, I meant it!'

'I think he believed you,' Captain Somercote said.

'He had better,' the Earl answered. 'I have spent no less than £25,000 on that young reprobate in the last two years. It is like throwing money down the drain.'

'Well, he has spent all that – and more!'

'Then he can go to the Fleet for all I care! I will not raise a finger to bail him out.'

'He has no intention of doing that.'

'Then what is he doing?'

'He is trying to marry a rich heiress!'

'Would he find one who would be such a fool as to have him?'

'That is exactly what I was going to talk to you about.

He has made himself a laughing-stock by trying to propose to every girl with money who appeared in London this Season.'

The Earl's lips tightened, but he said nothing.

His young cousin, Julius Lynd, had been a 'pain in the neck' ever since the Earl had inherited the title. He was a waster and a ne'er-do-well upon whom no amount of reprimand had any effect.

The Earl's father had had one younger brother who became an alcoholic and died from drink at an early age.

His widow consoled herself by spoiling their only child inordinately and Julius had grown up to create scandal after scandal and behave in a manner which made the Earl rage whenever he thought of him.

As he was the Earl's heir presumptive, he had made no pretence of not hoping his wounds at Waterloo would kill him, and had sulked when he was disappointed.

'Go on!' the Earl said sharply to Henry Somercote now, knowing there was more to come.

'Naturally Julius's reputation preceded him and the fathers of most of the heiresses chucked him out of the front door before he could even declare himself.'

Henry Somercote looked at the Earl warily as he went on :

'He was even caught in one young girl's bedroom trying to compromise her, and only escaped from being strangled by her father by shinning down a drainpipe.

'It makes me sick to hear about it!' the Earl said violently.

'I thought you would be none to pleased,' Captain Somercote said, 'but I ought to warn you that he is coming to Cheltenham. In fact I believe has has already arrived.'

'Coming here? What the hell for?' the Earl enquired.

'He is chasing a Miss Clutterbuck. I think she is his last hope. She is as plain as a pikestaff, and the wrong side of thirty-five. but her father, Ebenezer Clutterbuck, is an exceedingly rich man.'

He paused to say slowly and impressively:

'Usurers usually are!'

The Earl made a sound of sheer rage.

'Dammit all! I will not have a usurer's daughter in the family! The Lynds, for the last hundred years at any rate, have been respectable.'

'From all I hear, Miss Clutterbuck is likely to accept him. Despite her money she has not had many offers and Julius, for all his faults, is a gentleman.'

'By birth, if not behaviour!' the Earl said bitterly.

He was thinking to himself that here was another problem and one which would also have to be solved immediately.

'If I give Julius money,' he said aloud, as if he was voicing his thoughts, 'there is nothing to ensure he will not use it to pay off his debts and at the same time marry this Clutterbuck woman, if she is really rich.'

'It is infuriating for you, I know,' Henry Somercote said sympathetically. 'I am sorry to be the bearer of bad news, but I thought you ought to know what is going on.'

'I would rather know the worst,' the Earl conceded.

'If you ask me, someone ought to teach young Julius a sharp lesson,' Captain Somercote said.

'I agree,' the Earl replied, 'but it does not sound as if Ebenezer Clutterbuck is likely to do so.'

'Not he! He will jump at the chance of having an aristocratic son-in-law!'

Then suddenly Henry Somercote laughed.

'The whole thing is like one of those nonsensical dramas in which the Colonel likes to act. The reprobate nephew – Julius, an incensed guardian – you, the old Usurer licking his lips at the thought of moving in Society, and the ugly, doubtless pock-marked bride, who is really the unfortunate dupe.'

Henry Somercote laughed again, but there was a scowl on the Earl's face.

'All we need now,' he went on, 'is a heroine, a beautiful

Princess in disguise, who reforms the reprobate, so that all ends happily with wedding bells!'

The Earl sat upright.

'Henry, you have given me an idea.' he exclaimed. 'What is more, it will not only solve the problem of putting Julius in his place and saving the family from Miss Clutterbuck; it will also answer another problem, and an even more difficult one!'

3

'Ring the bell, Henry,' the Earl ordered.

'Why?'

'I will tell you about the idea you have given me,' the Earl replied, 'and I want Giselda to be here.'

Captain Somercote obliged by rising to his feet to tug at the embroidered bell-pull which hung beside the mantelshelf.

The door was opened almost immediately by Batley.

'You rang, M'Lord?'

'Fetch Miss Chart here!'

'Very good, M'Lord.'

'You are arousing my curiosity,' Henry Somercote said. 'You have that look about you as though something important is pending. I always knew in Portugal when you were anticipating a battle.'

The Earl laughed.

'I do not believe a word you are saying, he replied. 'At the same time I admit to having an engagement in mind.'

'And the enemy is Julius?'

'One of them!' the Earl remarked enigmatically.

Giselda came hurrying into the room.

'You wanted me?' she asked.

There was still that look of anxiety in her big eyes and a tautness in the lines of her mouth which the Earl had not seen since the first day they met.

'I want you to sit down, Giselda,' he said quietly, 'and listen to what I have to tell you. First of all, let me introduce an old friend, Captain Henry Somercote – Miss Giselda Chart.'

Giselda curtsied and Henry Somercote bowed.

Only when he saw the experession in her face did the Earl realise that she thought perhaps Henry Somercote was the man he had chosen to pay her the £50 she required.

Hastily, because the idea embarrassed him, he said:

'Captain Somercote, Giselda, has brought me news of a first cousin of mine, Julius Lynd, who is behaving in an extremely reprehensible manner.'

Giselda looked surprised, but she did not speak and the Earl went on:

'He is in fact, if I do not marry, heir to the title and as such I have certain responsibilities towards him.'

'No one could have treated him more generously than you have,' Captain Somercote interposed.

'Julius Lynd has already run through what would seem to you and most ordinary people a fortune,' the Earl continued, as if Henry Somercote had not spoken. 'I have paid up for him again and again, and now, quite frankly, I realise it is quite hopeless to pander to his extravagances.'

'The point is, Talbot,' Henry Somercote interposed again, 'Julius thinks you are an inexhaustible cornucopia, or shall we say a Bank whose reserves are completely at his disposal.'

'I agree it cannot go on,' the Earl said firmly.

Giselda's eyes were on his and he knew that she was puzzled as to how this should concern her.

'Henry has told me,' the Earl continued, 'that Julius, in order to make good his financial deficiencies, has pursued every heiress in London, and has now followed one here to Cheltenham.'

'You should see what she looks like,' Henry Somercote interrupted. 'I have seen many plain women in my life, but I have no doubt that if there was a competition for sheer ugliness Emily Clutterbuck would win it!'

For the first time Giselda seemed to relax a little and there was a faint smile on her lips.

'Clutterbuck?' she queried. 'What a surprising name!'

'She is the daughter of Ebenezer Clutterbuck, who is a moneylender,' the Earl said in a harsh tone.

He suddenly struck the bedclothes with his clenched fist.

'Dammit!' he swore. 'I have said it before and I will say it again – I will not have anyone called Clutterbuck in the family, nor will I countenance a cursed blood-sucking Usurer sitting at my table.'

'What can you do to prevent it?' Giselda asked quietly.

She rose from the chair as she spoke and tidied the lace-edged sheet which the Earl has crumpled.

Then she patted up the pillows behind him.

Henry Somercote watched her with amused eyes.

'Do not fuss!' the Earl commanded. 'I am trying to explain to you your part in this drama.'

'Mine?' Giselda enquired.

'Yes, yours,' the Earl replied. 'I presume you can act?'

Giselda looked bewildered and even Henry Somercote turned enquiring eyes towards the Earl.

'I intend to teach Julius a lesson he will not forget,' the Earl said grimly, 'and at the same time, Giselda, solve the problem with which you presented me a short time ago.'

She stared at him wide-eyed and the Earl went on:

'The only way to save Julius from the clutches of Miss Clutterbuck is to divert his attention to another heiress, who of course, must be equally rich, besides being attractive.'

There was silence for a moment in the bedroom. Then Giselda said in a hesitating tone:

'I .. I do not .. think I understand what you are .. suggesting.'

'I am telling you that you will be the heiress whom we will hold out as bait under Julius's nose to stop him pursuing this Clutterbuck woman.'

The Earl turned to look at Captain Somercote.

'You, Henry, will inform Julius how rich and important this alleged heiress is, and now I think of it, she had best come from the north — Yorkshire is a big County and as far as I know Julius has never been there.'

'But such an .. idea is .. impossible .. ' Giselda began.

'There is no such word as "impossible" in my vocabulary,' the Earl said loftily. 'Half the visitors to Cheltenham come from outlying parts of the country. Newell said so only yesterday in your presence. Therefore a rich heiress from Yorkshire will be merely one of the hundreds of people who wish to consult the doctors and drink the medicinal waters of the Spa.'

Henry Somercote rose to his feet.

'By Jove, Talbot, you are a genius at improvisation! I have always thought so, and so did the Duke! Do you remember how you turned the tide of that battle near Vittoria, when I was quite certain we were completely cut off by the French?'

'If we could beat the French, we can beat Julius at his own game!' the Earl said.

'But .. how can we .. make him think .. ' Giselda began helplessly.

'Leave everything to me,' the Earl said. 'You will be dressed as befits the part, and all you will have to do is to make yourself pleasant to Julius and let him think, in a very discreet way of course, that you are not averse to his paying court to you.'

'Oh .. I am sure I could not do it.'

'You will do it, and you will do it well!' the Earl said positively.

'It certainly is a most intriguing idea,' Henry Somercote said. 'Where is she to stay?'

There was a moment's pause as if the Earl was thinking.

'Here! I am damned if I am going to lose my nurse, and I am not going to miss all the fun and excitement.'

He laughed before he added:

'In which case I suppose we should ask the permission of Mine Host.'

'I am quite certain that Colonel Berkeley will enjoy every moment of the drama,' Henry Somercote said.

'What will I enjoy?' a voice asked from the door.

All three people in the bedroom turned their heads as Colonel Berkeley appeared.

'Talk of the devil!' he said, 'or am I cast in the part of the Demon King?'

His words were obviously addressed to Henry Somercote, but his eyes were on Giselda who rose to her feet as he advanced slowly into the room.

'You are just the man we want, Fitz.' the Earl remarked. 'We need your approval and your assistance in a proposition which is very much up your street.'

Colonel Berkeley had stopped beside Giselda.

'Will somebody introduce me?' he asked.

'Giselda, this is your host, Colonel Berkeley. Fitz – Miss Giselda Chart!'

Giselda curtsied.

'You are even more attractive than I thought when I had a quick glimpse of you,' Colonel Berkeley said.

The colour rose in Giselda's cheeks.

He looked at her for a long moment, and her eyes fell before his. He seated himself astride an upright chair, his arms crossed on the back of it.

'Now, tell me what is going on,' he said, 'for it is obvious that all three of you are conspiring.'

'That is exactly what we are doing,' the Earl replied.

Briefly he repeated what he had already said to Giselda and Colonel Berkeley laughed.

'Talk about the Cheltenham theatricals!' he said. 'My dear Talbot, I shall have you writing plays for me before I have finished.'

'There is no lead for you in this play,' the Earl retorted. 'Everything centres around Giselda. She has to convince

63

Julius that she is the heiress he will be told she is and thus make him stop pursuing Miss Clutterbuck and concentrate on the Yorkshire millions which he thinks might fall into his pocket.'

'Forsaking the substance for the shadow,' the Colonel remarked. 'Well, it certainly, my dear Talbot, has the making of a good First Act. More important, though, is what will happen in the other two.'

'The most important thing is for the play to be staged before Julius commits himself,' the Earl corrected.

'I agree with you there,' Henry Somercote said. 'When I left London everyone was expecting the engagement to be announced at any moment.'

'There is just a chance that Julius is shrewd enough to think that if he can frighten you, Talbot, by proposing such an alliance you will pay his debts. He has done this before,' Colonel Berkeley remarked.

'That is something I have no intention of doing!' the Earl retorted sharply.

'Then Giselda will have to be very convincing,' Colonel Berkeley replied.

He looked at her again in a manner which made her feel shy.

It had not escaped her notice that he had referred to her by her Christian name. Then she thought humbly she was after all only in the position of a servant and she could hardly expect these gentlemen to address her in any other way.

'Come on, Fitz,' the Earl prompted, 'this is where we need your expert advice!'

'Very well,' Colonel Berkeley said in a more serious tone. 'If Giselda is to be an heiress she had best be a widow. That will dispense with relatives who would undoubtedly try to keep Julius away from her, and also with the chaperonage she would otherwise require if she is to stay in this house.'

'Better make her a distant relative,' Henry Somercote

said. 'Otherwise you know the inference that might be put on her being a guest at German Cottage.'

The three men looked knowingly at each other, but the Earl was well aware that Giselda did not understand.

'If I am to be a widow,' she said, 'he might ask questions about my . . husband.'

'You can be too affected by the thought of his death to wish to talk about him,' the Colonel said. 'And for God's sake, do not forget that you will need a wedding ring.'

There was a sharpness in his voice which both the Earl and Henry Somercote knew came from the bitterness he felt at being illegitimate.

The case that had been heard in the House of Lords four years previously in 1812 had caused a tremendous sensation. Every possible evidence was brought by his mother to prove that Fitz had been born in wedlock.

But the House of Lords ruled that the Colonel's younger brother, Moreton, was in fact the Sixth Earl of Berkeley.

The judgement had made the Colonel behave in a wilder and more flamboyant manner than he had done before.

The publicity, the agonising ordeal suffered by his mother, and the details of the sensational hearing which had dragged on for nearly four months had left him resentful and at the same time defiant.

He would not admit that he had been humiliated, but the scars were to remain with him all through his life.

'Giselda will require not only a wedding ring,' the Earl said, 'but also clothes.'

'Yes, of course,' Colonel Berkeley said in a different tone, 'and that is where I can help you. Madame Vivienne, who dresses my theatrical productions is a genius. She will also keep her mouth shut, which is important. Otherwise the whole of Cheltenham will know that Giselda is being fitted out with a trousseau.'

'What about the servants? Especially if she stays here?' Henry asked.

The Colonel looked at him disdainfully.

'You do not suppose that any servants in my employment would dare to gossip about one of my guests, or indeed anything that goes on in this house?'

He paused to add impressively:

'The outside world may talk about me, but I assure you that what occurs in any house I own is completely private, except that there are always inquisitive fools who are prepared to believe the worst.'

'There is to be no guessing about Giselda,' the Earl said firmly. 'Send for this Madame Vivienne, and she must be dressed as befits an heiress. At the same time quietly and respectably as would be expected of a widow from Yorkshire.'

'Have you thought of a name for her?' Henry enquired.

There was silence as all three men seemed to be thinking. Then the Colonel spoke first:

'Barrowfield will do. I remember there was a character of that name in one of the first plays I ever acted in, and he, or she, I cannot remember which, was supposed to have come from Yorkshire.'

'Very well,' the Earl agreed, 'Giselda can be Mrs Barrowfield, widow of a Yorkshire Squire who made millions from wool.'

'Her mother can have been a distant cousin of mine,' the Colonel said, 'and that will eradicate any complication over names.'

Suddenly, as if the full implication of what was being planned swept over her, Giselda said in a frightened little voice:

'Please .. I am afraid .. of doing this ... Supposing I let you down? Supposing I am .. discovered?'

'Then Julius will marry Miss Clutterbuck,' Henry replied before anyone else could speak, 'and there will be no great harm done one way or the other. Mrs Barrowfield can disappear back to Yorkshire.'

He had taken it upon himself to answer Giselda's plea,

but she had been looking at the Earl and he knew she appealed to him for protection and reassurance.

'You will do it splendidly!' he said. 'And really you will have very little to do. Julius will come to call on me, I am quite certain, once Henry has told him that an heiress is staying in the house. You will be introduced and some-how – we must play this by ear – he will suggest that he accompanies you to the Spa, and he may after a few casual meetings invite you to dinner.'

He realised as he spoke that the very idea made Giselda afraid, and he told himself all that really mattered was that this solved her problem as well as his own.

'I have an idea,' the Colonel said. 'Knightley has in his charge a collection of jewellery which I use in my pro-ductions.'

He looked at Giselda and added as if he sensed her nervousness at wearing anything valuable:

'The stones are only semi-precious – garnets, amethysts, and I believe there is a small string of pearls. It would seem strange for an heiress to possess no jewellery of any sort.'

'Yes, of course,' the Earl agreed. 'Really, Fitz, it will be impossible to put on this production without your help. How soon do you think Madame Vivienne can equip Giselda so that she can take the stage?'

'Immediately, I should think,' the Colonel replied lightly. 'And because I realise it is urgent, Talbot, I will go and see her myself and tell her to come here with all possible speed. She is sure to have a few gowns ready, enough at any rate for Giselda to make her first appear-ance.'

He smiled as he added to Giselda:

'That is the important moment! You have to evoke the interest of the audience and hold it for the rest of the play.'

Giselda made a convulsive little movement and he added:

'No "First Night nerves"! I never allow my players to suffer from them. All I ask is that they should know their lines and do exactly as I have told them to do.'

'It is not knowing my .. lines which makes me so .. nervous,' Giselda said.

'Leave everything to me,' the Colonel answered in an almost caressing tone. 'I will produce you, Giselda, and I can assure you I am very experienced at it.'

'I .. think I would .. rather leave that to .. His Lordship,' Giselda said in a low voice.

The Earl could not help feeling a sense of triumph that she preferred to rely on him rather than on the Colonel.

But if it was meant to be a set-down the Colonel was not prepared to take it as one.

'Of course,' he agreed. 'This is Talbot's play and I must not spoil his sense of the dramatic. At the same time I hereby appoint myself as Stage Manager, and quite frankly, without being conceited, I am an extremely good one.'

'We all know that,' the Earl said, 'but you are not to frighten Giselda. I am quite certain she has never done anything like this before and it will not be easy for her.'

'Who knows, we may have another Mrs Jordan or Harriet Melon on our hands,' Colonel Berkeley remarked.

'Or even a Maria Foote!' Henry Somercote said slyly.

The Colonel looked at him and he added:

'I saw her in *A Roland for an Oliver*, and I thought she was superb!'

'She is very beautiful,' the Colonel said complacently as if he was responsible for it.

'Giselda will make an adequate Mrs Barrowfield,' the Earl said, 'and that is all we require of her at the moment. Hurry, Fitz, and find Madame Vivienne for me, and you Henry, see if you can discover where Julius is staying.'

'He is staying at The Plough, and Miss Clutterbuck is at The Swan.'

'Then let us hope we can keep them apart.'

Henry Somercote leant against the foot of the bed.

'What exactly do you want me to stay to him?'

The Earl paused for a moment, then said slowly:

'Tell him you have been to see me and that I am in good health. Then rave about the charming and delightful widow who is also staying at German Cottage.'

He paused a moment to say:

'Now I think of it, Giselda had better say when she gets the chance that she was accompanied from Yorkshire by an elderly aunt who was unfortunately taken ill and forced to stay in London, but will be joining her later.'

'A good idea!' the Colonel approved. 'Always make your characters have a reason for everything they do. It is part of the credibility that should be present in every play.'

'And then?' Henry prompted.

'Suggest, casually of course, that you are calling on me later this evening and that he should accompany you . . '

The Earl broke off to turn to the Colonel:

'Could Madame Vivienne have Giselda ready by then? Surely she will have at least one gown that will fit her?'

'I imagine there will be dozens,' the Colonel replied. 'Each one on Giselda more becoming than the last. Leave everything to me, Talbot! I am going straight away to find Madame Vivienne, and I will also speak to Knightley before I leave the house.'

'I will come with you,' Henry said. 'I feel sure there are a number of details in this important production that we should discuss together.'

'I will give you a lift,' the Colonel smiled. 'I have my Phaeton outside.'

'Thank you,' Henry replied. 'The trouble about this town of yours, Colonel, is that there is too much walking.'

'All the doctors will tell you that it is good for your health,' the Colonel replied.

'And I am quite certain you are thinking out some way by which you can charge people for every footstep they take,' Henry laughed.

The two men went from the bedroom and the Earl waited his eyes on Giselda.

He knew she was apprehensive. He knew too by the expression in her eyes that she could hardly believe this was not some fantasy that would never be put into action.

She moved towards the bed and stood holding on to the carved post at the foot of it as if she needed support.

'Do not be afraid, Giselda,' the Earl said gently, 'and I will write you now a cheque for the £50 you need so urgently.'

'It is too much!' she said. 'I am sure it is too much!'

'If you think that, you can ask the Colonel what he pays the amateurs who act for him,' the Earl replied. 'You will find that he gives them as much as that a week, and since I envisage this masquerade may continue for ten days or more I am really getting you on the cheap.'

He saw she was still unconvinced and said:

'You have obviously not heard the story of Edmund Kean who was paid £50 in Cheltenham for a morning performance, £50 in Tewkesbury in the afternoon, and again the same sum at Gloucester in the evening, so that he earned £150 in a day.'

'I am not .. Edmund Kean.'

The Earl smiled.

'Must I say the obvious?'

'You are .. only doing this to .. save me,' Giselda said hesitatingly.

'That is certainly half the reason why I suggested such a scheme,' the Earl admitted. 'The other half, as you are well aware, is because I do not want a Usurer's daughter as a close relative.'

'S . supposing Mr Lynd is not .. interested in me?'

'I have never suggested that he should be interested in you as a person,' the Earl replied, 'but he will undoubtedly be interested in your supposed money. Captain Somercote was not exaggerating when he said Julius has been pursuing every heiress during the Season in London and making every possible attempt to marry one of them.'

He wondered if he should tell Giselda of Julius's attempt to compromise a young girl and how he had had to escape down a drainpipe.

Then he told himself that it would only shock her, though she might in fact not understand exactly what was implied.

The only difficulty about this whole scheme, the Earl thought, was whether anyone would credit that Giselda was a married woman.

There was something very young and innocent about her; something which the Earl had certainly not found amongst the women with whom he had flirted and enjoyed himself before he was wounded.

In her plain blue gown she looked at the moment exactly what she was; a young girl bewildered by life and ignorant of all the subtleties and the intrigues of the fashionable world.

Then he told himself that the only alternative to what he had suggested was Giselda's own idea, the thought of which was something he could not contemplate.

In a voice that was authoritative because he knew she would obey it he said :

'Go downstairs, Giselda, and ask Mr Knightley for notes to the sum of £50. Tell him I will have a cheque ready when he wishes to collect it. You can take the money first thing tomorrow morning to Mr Newell and arrange for your brother's operation on Thusday.'

Giselda drew in her breath and for a moment there was a light in her eyes, then she said :

'If I fail you . . if Mr Lynd is not interested in me . . I should give it back.'

'If you argue with me,' the Earl said, 'I shall have a relapse and Newell will not be operating on anyone because he will be attending to me. For God's sake, girl, stop making difficulties and do what I tell you to do !'

He spoke angrily and Giselda moved a little nearer to him.

'I am .. sorry. I am upsetting you and it is the last thing I intended to do. I am grateful .. more grateful than I can ever say.'

'Then show your gratitude by doing your best in a part that should come quite naturally to you, that of being a lady, which you are by birth.'

'. . . . and a servant by profession,' Giselda added with a smile.

'I look upon you as my Nurse,' the Earl said, 'and however grand you may become in your new clothes, however many Balls and Assemblies you attend in the person of Mrs Barrowfield, you will attend to my leg and pander to my every wish whenever you are off duty.'

'You know I .. want to do that,' Giselda said softly, 'and please .. may I thank you again?'

There was something very gentle in her voice and the expression in her eyes which the Earl had not seen there before.

Then because he knew it was the best way to deal with her, and because he was unexpectedly afraid of responding, he said sharply :

'I have no intention of being neglected.'

'You will not be,' Giselda promised, 'but I am sure now that you should rest.'

'I will rest as long as I am not kept in ignorance of what is going on,' the Earl said. 'When Madame Vivienne arrives I wish to see her and tell her what I require. I will choose your gowns myself, one by one.'

'Yes, of course,' Giselda agreed. Then a sudden thought struck her.

'Will .. will you be .. paying for them?'

'I shall be paying for them!' the Earl said positively. 'And I do not want any argument about it, Giselda. No one can put on a stage-show without it costing money, and I assure you that anything expended on your behalf will be very much less than what Julius has cost me this last year, let alone the sums I have coughed up in previous years.'

'How can he possibly spend so much money? What does he buy with it?' Giselda enquired.

'If I could answer "horses", which would be true of the Colonel who spends a fortune on his, there would be some excuse,' the Earl replied. 'But Julius's money goes on drink and women, and of course on gambling.'

'How foolish!'

'As you say, very foolish and very expensive!'

'I could never admire a man who was a gambler,' Giselda said reflectively. 'There is something so nonsensical in wagering money, especially if you cannot afford it, on the turn of a card.'

'And what about the other vices?' the Earl asked, 'women for instance?'

To his surprise the colour rose in Giselda's face and her eyes, that had been looking frankly into his, dropped.

'In some .. cases,' she said in a hard little voice that the Earl had never heard before, 'such behaviour is .. indefensible.'

She rose as she spoke and walked towards the door.

'I will tell the Butler that when Madame Vivienne comes you wish to see her,' she said, and left the room.

The Earl stared after her in surprise.

So among all the other mysteries there was something connected with women of the type he had insinuated which upset her.

He wondered if perhaps her father had left her and her family destitute because of some 'fancy woman' who proved more attractive than domesticity.

Perhaps that was the solution, but if it was why should she be so very secretive about it?

It was a situation that had happened thousands of times, and usually those who were left behind were resentful and very vocal in their resentment.

73

Mysteries — always more mysteries!

And the Earl realised that he was still no nearer to solving any of them than he had been when Giselda had first intrigued him because she was starving.

Well, she was certainly not starving now, and he imagined that her family, although they would not be living in luxury, would not be hungry either on the £1 a week she earned and the fact that she took food home for them.

Now her brother could have his operation.

'I suppose I am learning a little more about her than I knew at first,' the Earl told himself.

He recalled how much easier it had been in the war to discover information about the enemy than it was to discover anything about Giselda.

Then there had been spies to tell him what he wanted to know, the interrogation of prisoners and a dozen other ways which kept him the best informed Commander in the whole of the Peninsula.

Despite the fact that he had so much to think about, he did in fact, after a light luncheon, doze a little to awaken with a start when Madame Vivienne was shown into the bedroom.

A vivacious Frenchwoman, she had concealed her nationality during the war, but was now prepared to proclaim it to the world.

The Earl discovered that Madame Vivienne had worked for the Colonel ever since he had produced his first play.

She had already been briefed by him in what was required.

She informed the Earl that she had brought with her all the gowns she had ready, with bonnets and shawls to go with them, besides some sketches and patterns of material for him to make a selection of other gowns.

The sketches and patterns were placed on the bed while Madame Vivienne suggested that she should take Giselda into another room and dress her in a gown she had brought with her.

'I understand, *Milor*, there is a special occasion and a special gentleman this evening for whom Mrs Barrowfield must look her best.'

Both the Earl and Giselda found it hard for a moment to remember of whom the dressmaker was speaking.

Then Madame Vivienne whisked Giselda away and the Earl was left looking at the sketches, most of which he considered too theatrical and flamboyant for Giselda's quiet, unassuming personality.

He was however to change his mind and receive a shock a little later.

He had begun to wonder what could be happening in the other room and was considering ringing for Batley to take a message that he was tired of waiting when the door opened and Madame Vivienne came in.

'I have dressed Mrs Barrowfield,' she said to the Earl, 'exactly as *Monsieur Le Colonel* instructed me. I hope, *Milor*, it meets with your approval.'

She made a gesture with her hand and Giselda, as if she had actually been waiting in the wings of a theatre came slowly into the room.

The Earl could only stare at her in astonishment.

Madame Vivienne's instructions had been explicit and she had carried out the Colonel's orders to the letter.

Giselda looked older than her nineteen years and certainly more opulent, but the Earl had not expected that she would look so beautiful.

For a moment he could not understand what had happened to change her appearance so dramatically.

Then he understood.

Madame Vivienne had applied to Giselda's face the fashionable cosmetics that were used by all the ladies of the *Beau Monde* – not as vividly as those employed by the theatrical profession, but delicately as a Lady of Quality would use them.

And for the first time the Earl realised why Giselda, except for the largeness of her eyes, had seemed so pale and insignificant. She had used no cosmetics for the obvious reason that she could not afford them.

Now her white skin seemed to glow with the translucence of a pearl and there was a faint flush on her cheeks which concealed the hollows under her cheek-bones.

Her eyes seemed to have a new luminosity about them, while her eyelashes looked very long, dark and silky.

There was a touch of lip-salve on her curving mouth and her hair had been arranged in a corona on top of her head with ringlets which fell on either side of her small face.

Her gown was outstandingly fashionable, but at the same time not too exaggerated for a lady, although it was more elaborate and sophisticated than the type of gown that would have been worn by a girl of nineteen.

The Earl stared, then realised that both women were waiting for his verdict. With his eyes still on Giselda, he said:

'I can only congratulate you, *Madame*. The Colonel was right. You are an *artiste*, and may I say I think you have produced a masterpiece!'

Madame Vivienne swept him a curtsey.

'*Merci, Milor*, if you are satisfied then that is all I ask.'

'I am very satisfied!' the Earl said positively.

.   .   .   .   .

It was growing late in the afternoon before Madame Vivienne left and Giselda came into the room alone.

'I am . . worried,' she said.

'Why?' the Earl asked.

'When *Madame* came and saw you alone she said you had instructed her to buy me dozens of gowns. Really . . I do not need so many . . and the bill will be enormous!'

'Are you interfering with my arrangements, Giselda?' the Earl enquired.

'No . . no, of course not,' she replied. 'It is just that I do not wish you to .. spend so much money on .. me.'

'I can spend my money how I wish,' the Earl answered, 'and I would like to point out to you that I have had very little opportunity of spending a penny of my very considerable fortune this last year except on doctors who, with the exception of Newell, showed little return for my guineas.'

'You mean .. you enjoy buying the gowns you have chosen for me .. and all the other things?'

'I am speaking the truth when I tell you that I have enjoyed it very much!' the Earl answered. 'And shall I use a rather banal phrase and say that you "pay with dressing"?'

She still looked troubled and after a moment he said:

'If you talk of paying me back, I think I shall spank you! However, if it salves that tiresome, irritating pride of yours, let me say that, if you decide you have no further use for the clothes or if we quarrel unaccountably over some trifle such as extravagance, then we can give the gowns to the Colonel's theatrical wardrobe.'

The Earl paused to go on:

'I have learnt from Madame Vivienne that he has a considerable stock of garments of all sorts and of all periods, so that if he wishes to do so, he can put on a production at a moment's notice.'

He smiled as he went on:

'I am told that there are fast horses and carriages kept especially in Cheltenham ready to convey anything he requires for the charades and theatricals which often take place at Berkeley Castle.'

'I s . suppose you think I am very .. foolish,' Giselda said in a low voice.

'On the contrary,' the Earl replied, 'I respect your feelings in this matter. Most women are only too ready to grab anything that can be got from a man. You are the exception, Giselda, and I think many men would find it one of your most endearing qualities.'

He saw her give a little sigh of relief. Then she said, almost like a child who wishes to be reassured:

'I will not .. fail you .. will I?'

'I am quite sure you could never do that,' the Earl said.

He spoke in an unexpectedly deep voice. Then as his eyes met Giselda's something strange seemed to pass between them.

For a moment they were both very still. Then Giselda turned away to say a little incoherently:

'I .. I will .. ring for your .. tea .. or would you .. prefer something .. stronger?'

'I think we both need a glass of wine,' the Earl replied. 'I because I shall enjoy it, and you because, as you well know, Henry may bring Julius here at any moment.'

He saw a little quiver go through her. Then she looked at him and he knew without being told that she was thinking of what had just passed between them when he had told her that he knew she would not fail him.

'At least I have solved her problem,' the Earl told himself.

He wondered why he disliked, almost violently, the thought that to justify the £50 she would have to spend her time with Julius.

*   *   *   *   *

Although he was tired and he was in fact suffering no pain in his leg the Earl found it difficult to sleep.

He could not help going over and over again all that had happened earlier in the evening when Henry, as he had expected, had brought Julius to call on him.

As soon as Batley announced that the gentlemen were downstairs Giselda had slipped from the room and the Earl received Henry Somercote and Julius alone.

'This is a surprise, Julius!' he said to his young cousin with an affability he had seldom shown in the past.

'I am glad to see you are better, Cousin Talbot.'

Henry Somercote was a 'Tulip of Fashion', but Julius failed in his attempts to emulate one.

He was expensively dressed, but he had neither the physique nor the character of the two older men who had been in the Army, nor had he the good taste for which Henry Somercote was famous.

His pantaloons were not the perfect shade of yellow which had been made fashionable by the Regent; his cravat was just a little too frilled; and the points of his collar were a trifle too high for them not to appear exaggerated.

Yet to a woman's eyes, the Earl thought almost savagely, Julius would appear a very presentable young man.

It was only when one looked at the lines under his eyes and the slight thickening under his chin that one realised he was not in particularly good shape for a young man of twenty-four.

But there was no criticism in His Lordship's expression or in his voice as he asked his guests to sit down and sent for more wine.

'I was having a glass by myself,' he explained, 'and I am hoping you will join me, and I have also invited another guest who is staying in the house, a Mrs Barrowfield. I have not yet had an answer. She may have another engagement.'

He saw without appearing to do so that Julius's face fell.

'I have been telling Julius about Mrs Barrowfield,' Henry Somercote said conversationally. 'When I met her here yesterday I thought her extremely attractive!'

'I am afraid I do not think so myself,' the Earl replied coldly, 'although there are obviously a large number of ardent gentlemen like yourself who do so.'

'That is not surprising when you remember how much Barrowfield left,' Henry Somercote remarked.

'Was she very much younger than her husband?' Julius enquired.

'I believe much younger,' Henry Somercote replied. 'I think it was his second marriage, although I am not sure. Anyway she is young to be a widow, and who will quarrel with that when she has the Barrowfield millions behind her?'

'I have never heard of the Barrowfields,' Julius said in a peevish manner, as if he had somehow been deprived of such knowledge. 'Do you know anything about them, Cousin Talbot?'

'Not heard of the Barrowfields?' the Earl repeated in a voice of incredulity. 'My dear boy ..!'

There was no reason to say more, or, the Earl thought, to lie. It was obvious that Julius was convinced that Mrs Barrowfield was all that Henry Somercote had said she was.

The door opened.

'Mrs Barrowfield, M'Lord!' Batley announced and Giselda came into the room.

The Earl held out his hand.

'How very kind of you to give me the pleasure of your company,' he said in his most charming voice. 'I was afraid you might have a more interesting engagement than visiting an invalid.'

'It is .. kind of you to .. ask me,' Giselda answered.

She put her hand as she spoke into the Earl's and he felt her fingers were very cold and trembling with nervousness, and he held them closer hoping to give her confidence.

'You must let me introduce my other guests,' he said. 'Captain Henry Somercote you met yesterday, and this is my young cousin, Mr Julius Lynd, who has only just arrived from London. He will be able to acquaint us with all the news we miss in this quiet watering-place.'

Giselda smiled at both gentlemen shyly, then seated herself on the chair nearest to the bed.

The Earl noted that Mr Knightley had produced the jewellery of which the Colonel had spoken.

Giselda wore the single string of pearls round her neck, a pretty brooch of amethysts to her bodice, and an amethyst and pearl ring on the third finger of her left hand on which there was also a gold wedding ring.

'Have you been to Cheltenham before, Mrs Barrowfield?' Julius asked.

He was sitting on the chair next to Giselda and he leant forward eagerly.

'No, this is my first visit,' Giselda replied. 'I was so excited when Colonel Berkeley invited my aunt and myself to be his guests. We had heard so much of the beauty of Cheltenham and the efficacy of its waters.'

'And you will be taking them yourself?' Julius enquired.

'I expect to, although I do not think I really need them,' Giselda answered with a faint smile. 'But my aunt urgently requires their medicinal qualities. Unfortunately, she was taken ill when we reached London and will not be joining me for a few days.'

'Then if, until she arrives, you have no one to escort you to the Pump Room,' Julius said, 'I hope you will allow me to show you the way there, and introduce you to Mrs Forty, who is one of the characters of Cheltenham.'

Giselda looked at him enquiringly and he explained:

'Mrs Forty is a well-known pumper who served the King and Queen and the Royal Family when they came here and whose portrait was painted at His Majesty's command.'

Julius had this off so pat that the Earl was sure he had looked it up in a Guide book before calling, so that he could, if necessary, impress the rich Mrs Barrowfield with his knowledge of Cheltenham.

Henry Somercote must have done his work well, the Earl thought, and avoided his friend's eye in case he should laugh.

'It would certainly be very interesting to meet Mrs Forty,' Giselda said.

'Then may I effect the introduction tomorrow morning?' Julius asked. 'At what time do you wish to take the waters?'

'I should think that ten o'clock would be early enough.'

'That is the fashionable hour,' Henry Somercote said, 'and you will find all the notabilities of Cheltenham sipping away and pretending that the water is doing them good, while really they think it is disgusting.'

'Is it really so nasty?' Giselda enquired.

'I have not the slightest idea,' Henry Somercote replied. 'I have never tasted it and have no intention of doing so, but I certainly think that Talbot should go to the Pump as soon as he is well enough.'

'Let me make it quite clear — I have no intention of drinking the water!' the Earl said firmly.

He glanced at Giselda as he spoke and thought there was a little glint in her eye that told him that if she thought it would do him good she would certainly try to persuade him to try it.

He could see a battle ahead and felt amused at the thought of it.

'There are many other things I can show you, Mrs Barrowfield,' Julius was saying. 'The Assembly Rooms are delightful and the theatre is to have a special play for the Duke of Wellington's visit entitled *Love in a Village*.'

'Will there be anyone famous playing in it?' Giselda asked, since it was obvious that she was expected to say something.

'I have no idea,' Julius was forced to admit.

'Perhaps Maria Foote will have a leading part,' Henry Somercote interposed.

But if she did he and the Earl knew the reason for it.

Julius went on talking, but it was obvious that while he was doing his best to ingratiate himself with the 'rich widow' he was somewhat restricted by the fact that he was also being listened to and watched by his cousin and Guardian.

Occasionally he looked at the Earl with an expression

of defiance in his eyes, but His Lordship continued to be affable.

There was no doubt that by the end of his visit, if Julius Lynd was apprehensive as to the Earl's feelings towards him, they had been assuaged.

He had in fact been rather afraid that the Earl would learn not only of his pursuit of women but also the fact that he had in the past year borrowed a considerable sum of money on his expectations of succeeding to the title.

Although he was paying an enormous rate of interest, there had seemed to be every chance that the Earl would die of his wounds and therefore he would be able to pay back the loan much more quickly than anyone might have anticipated.

But he had only to look at his cousin now to realise that he was well on the way to recovery!

Although outwardly Julius was pleasant and polite he cursed the fact that the Earl had been persuaded to visit Cheltenham to be operated on by Thomas Newell, one of the most famous Surgeons in the country.

By all the laws of good fortune, Julius told himself, Cousin Tabot should have been killed at Waterloo, or at least died because he would not have his leg amputated.

The Earl had been spoken of as being quite a hero in his defiance of the Regimental doctors and refusal, even when he was running a high fever from the festering of the grapeshot, to listen to their advice.

And yet with his usual, unbelievable luck the risk had paid off, and now it seemed to Julius that it could be forty years or more before he had a chance of succeeding to the Earldom.

Cursing the fate that had played him such a scurvy trick he was wondering as he talked to Giselda whether he would be wise to transfer his attentions from Emily Clutterbuck to this far more attractive woman, who according to Henry Somercote, had a much greater fortune and a decidedly more attractive background.

At the same time, Emily was, to put it vulgarly, 'in the bag!'

She had made it quite clear that she welcomed his advances, and the fact that he had followed her to Cheltenham would, he knew, make it very plain what his intentions were.

The thought of Ebenezer Clutterbuck as a father-in-law made him feel sick, and Emily herself was so unprepossessing, besides being twelve years older than he was himself, that the mere idea of marriage to her was nauseating.

But his debtors were waiting to pounce on him and his debts, despite the money he had received from his cousin this past year, were astronomical.

It was impossible for him to go on as he was or to give up the only type of life he understood.

Once Emily was his wife there would be plenty of money to pay for the hundreds of 'fair charmers' who would be only too willing to make him forget that he was a married man.

At the same time Julius thought craftily that if it was a case of 'penny plain or twopence coloured', who was he to hesitate?

There was no doubt in his mind that everything would be easier in every way if the Lynd family, and especially the Earl himself, accepted his choice of a wife.

There would be no difficulties where Mrs Barrowfield was concerned, but he could imagine all too vividly what their reactions would be to poor Emily!

When Giselda rose to say that she was going to her room to rest before dinner Julius rose too.

He had made up his mind.

'I was always a gambler,' he told himself.

When he said good-bye to Giselda he held her hand a little longer than was necessary and told her in a voice that was overwhelmingly sincere that he was counting the hours until ten o'clock tomorrow morning.

'You are very kind, Sir,' Giselda said as she curtsied.

With an excess of gallantry Julius raised her hand to his lips.

She moved away from him down the long passage towards another large guest room which had now been allotted to her by Mrs Kingdom.

Later, by peeping over the banisters, she saw the front door close behind Julius and ran back to the Earl's bedroom.

She ran in impetuously, and ignoring Henry Somercote who was saying good-bye to the Earl she put out both her hands towards him.

'Was I .. all right?' she asked. 'Did I do what you wanted me to do? Do you think he was convinced?'

'You were perfection!' the Earl said quietly.

4

'Goodnight, Mrs Barrowfield.'

'Goodnight, Mr Lynd, and thank you very much for escorting me this evening.'

'The pleasure has been entirely mine,' Julius replied. 'I only wish we could have had more time *together*.'

There was no doubting the stress on the last word and as he spoke he took Giselda's hand in his and held it very closely.

As Giselda wondered what she should reply, he went on in a low voice:

'There is so much I want to say to you and I did hope I should have a chance this evening.'

Apprehensively Giselda looked over her shoulder at the Butler and footmen standing in the hall behind them and at the same time took her hand from his.

There was no need for her to say anything – he knew what she was thinking.

'Allow me tomorrow,' Julius said, 'to call for you at ten o'clock to take you to the Pump.'

He bent his head and kissed her hand, and she could feel the warm pressure of his lips through the thin lace mittens she wore.

With what was a considerable effort she forced herself to murmur:

'Thank you once again . . and now I must . . go.'

She managed to extract her hand and move quickly up the steps and into the hall.

Although she did not look back she felt that Julius was standing watching her, and only when she was halfway up the stairs and heard the front door shut firmly did she feel free of him.

Resisting an impulse to rub her hand where his lips had lingered, she moved even quicker up the stairs to the landing and only paused when she was outside the Earl's bedchamber.

'Perhaps he will be asleep,' she thought.

But he had been insistent before she left that she should come in and see him when she returned from the Assembly Rooms where Julius had taken her.

Very softly Giselda turned the handle and opened the door. Then she saw the candles were alight beside the big four-poster, and the Earl was sitting up in bed obviously awake.

She came into the room, closed the door behind her and was halfway towards him before he said :

'You are very late !'

There was an accusing note in his voice and Giselda answered quickly :

'I am sorry. It was impossible to get away sooner.'

'What do you mean – impossible ?'

'There was so much to .. see and .. Colonel Berkeley introduced me to a number of people.'

'Why did he do that ?'

'I think he meant to be kind, and also to impress on everybody that I was in fact a relative.'

Giselda reached the bedside to stand looking at the Earl.

She was looking very lovely, as indeed he had thought before she set out.

She was wearing a gown of pale pink gauze, scalloped round the hem with tiny frills of lace which also ornamented the bodice and sleeves.

Round her neck she wore a small necklace of aquamarines which seemed to echo the blue of her eyes.

'Tell me what happened and what you thought of the Assembly Rooms,' the Earl said.

'They seemed to be very attractive,' Giselda answered. 'But everyone was talking about the new rooms and disparaging the old.'

She gave a faint smile and said:

'Apparently, because they have to close, the rules were relaxed for this evening.'

'What rules?' the Earl enquired.

'Colonel Berkeley told me that no hazard or games of chance were permitted in the Rooms, but tonight some of the ladies and gentlemen were playing écarté.'

There was a little pause, before Giselda said:

'I did not .. know what I .. should do.'

'What do you mean by that?' the Earl enquired.

'Colonel Berkeley suggested that I should play and of course I began to say "no", but he would not listen. "I will be your banker", he said, "and it is well known that when a lovely lady plays for the first time she always wins"!'

Giselda made a little gesture with her hands.

'He made it impossible for me to refuse him, and in any case, I thought that if I seemed too reluctant Mr Lynd would not think I was as .. rich as I am .. pretending to be.'

'I can understand your difficulty,' the Earl said.

'I won,' Giselda went on. 'At least the Colonel told me I had, but I could not really understand the game.'

'How much did you win?'

'Ten guineas.'

Giselda raised her eyes to the Earl's.

'What am I to do? He would not let me refuse to take it and it seemed nonsensical for me to make a great fuss when Mr Lynd thinks I am so wealthy.'

'And what did you do?' the Earl asked.

'I brought it back with me,' Giselda answered.

She put her little satin reticule down on the sheets in front of the Earl.

'I see no difficulty about this,' he said. 'The money is

yours, though I suspect that Colonel Berkeley was being generous since he has some idea of your real circumstances.'

'I do not .. wish to take .. favours from the .. Colonel.'

There was something in Giselda's tone which made the Earl look at her sharply. However he did not speak the words which rose to his lips, but said:

'The money is yours, Giselda, and I am sure you can make good use of it.'

'I want to give it to .. you,' Giselda said. 'You have spent so .. much on my clothes and you have been so kind to me.'

The Earl stared at her incredulously for a moment. Then he said:

'Are you really trying to reimburse me in a manner which I should consider an insult?'

'No .. no, please do not feel like .. that!' Giselda pleaded. 'It is only that it is such a large sum and I can never repay you what I owe.'

'You owe me nothing,' the Earl said firmly. 'You are helping me personally, even if at the same time you are helping yourself. Henry told me today that Miss Clutterbuck seems completely disillusioned by the way Julius is behaving and he fancies she will soon be leaving Cheltenham. When that happens our masquerade is at an end.'

He picked up the little satin bag as he spoke, shook it, heard the jingle of the guineas inside it, and handed it to Giselda.

'Look on this as being in the way of a Benefit for your extremely clever performance.'

He smiled as he added:

'All actors and actresses expect to have a Benefit. In fact the majority live on them, so why should you be the exception?'

'You really think it is .. right for me to .. accept this money?'

'I shall be very angry with you if you refuse to do so,'

the Earl said. 'It will be, as you well know, a Godsend when your brother comes home. How long does Mr Newell consider keeping him?'

'He said as the operation was so serious he would have to stay in Hospital until the end of the week.'

'But it was successful?'

'So we all .. believe,' Giselda said in a breathless voice. 'If you only knew how grateful Mama and I are to you for making it possible.'

'You are the person who made it possible,' the Earl answered. 'But as you say, Rupert will need careful looking after when he is convalescent and, as you will not let me help, then you have in your usual clever fashion managed to help yourself.'

Giselda took the reticule from him and as she did not reply the Earl said quietly:

'I think it is very un-Christian of you to prevent me from acquiring some merit by helping your family. Have you not read in your Bible that it is "more blessed to give than to receive"?'

'You have already given me .. everything I want.'

'But not much as I should like to give you,' the Earl insisted. 'You are still, Giselda, treating me as if I were an enemy.'

'No, no, never that!' she said. 'It is just..'

Her voice died away and the Earl after a moment said grimly:

'It is just that there are secrets that you will not reveal to me – in fact you do not trust me. I find that very hurtful.'

'I .. want to trust you .. I promise you I do .. but I cannot,' Giselda answered.

There was a note almost like a sob in her voice, and after a moment the Earl said:

'I think you are tired, so I will not plague you any more tonight. Go to bed, Giselda. Put your golden guineas under your pillow where they will be safe, and be quite certain in your own mind that you are entitled to every one of them.'

'You are quite comfortable .. you are not in any pain?'

'My leg, as you well know, is almost healed,' the Earl replied, 'and if I worry about anything it will not be about myself – but you!'

'There is no reason for you to worry about me.'

'How can I be sure of that when you are so mysterious – so secretive? When you erect a barrier between us which I find impregnable?'

'I do not .. mean to be like .. that,' Giselda said, 'I wish ..'

Again her voice died away as if she was afraid of saying any more, and she turned towards the door.

When she reached it she curtsied and it was a very graceful gesture.

'Goodnight, My Lord,' she said softly, 'and thank you from the bottom of my heart.'

She went from the room, but the Earl sat staring at the closed door for a long time.

He was trying, as he had tried a thousand times before, to imagine what was the mystery that Giselda hid so determinedly from him.

He had hoped that sooner or later she would trust him and tell him about herself, so he had told Batley to make no more enquiries about her.

He merely tried to piece together like a puzzle the few pieces of information that Giselda let drop from time to time in her conversation.

He knew that she had lived in the country, but she was well educated and he fancied, although he was not sure, that she had also at one time lived in London.

He had tried to get her to talk about her mother; but she either answered his questions in monosyllables, or refused to answer them at all.

He knew that she adored her small brother – but that was all!

Although the Earl might have asked questions of Thomas Newell, he deliberately refrained from doing so. However curious he might be, he still had a respect for Giselda's reticence, he told himself, and would not spy upon her in an underhand manner.

At the same time he found it more and more frustrating to realise that he was failing in what he felt was a battle of wills between them.

He also resented, although he would hardly dare admit it to himself, the fact that Giselda should do things with Julius, and apparently with Colonel Berkeley also, without his being able to accompany her.

He had disliked the thought of her visiting the Assembly Rooms this evening. But it was impossible for Giselda to refuse Julius's invitations and it would in fact have seemed strange for Mrs Barrowfield not to wish to inspect the centre of all the entertainment which took place in Cheltenham.

The Earl however had felt it was one thing for her to visit the Pump Rooms and drink the waters, but quite different to dance at night in the Assembly Rooms.

'I have no wish to go,' Giselda had said.

'You will enjoy it,' Henry Somercote who was there at the time answered. 'Good gracious, you are only young once! Even His Lordship cannot expect you to go on bandaging interminably either his leg or somebody else's until you are too old to receive any invitations.'

'I cannot think Julius is a particularly desirable partner with whom Giselda should make her début,' the Earl said scathingly.

'Needs must when the devil drives!' Henry Somercote said cheerfully. 'Giselda need not listen to Julius's protestations of affection, knowing exactly how much they are worth.'

He called Giselda by her Christian name just as the Earl did. In fact, Giselda thought of them as two elderly Guardians concerned with her welfare, at the same time forced by circumstances to allow her a licence of behaviour which they would not normally have done.

She only wished as she set out in the evening that she had another escort than Julius Lynd.

She had soon realised that everything the Colonel and Henry Somercote had said about him was true and that under a polished superficial veneer he was in fact a very unpleasant young man.

He was too suave, too plausible, and above all, she told herself, when he smiled his eyes did not smile too.

Then after two or three days' acquaintance she began to fancy, although she thought she might be mistaken, that his manner towards her was changing.

He had begun, because he thought her rich, by trying to be very impressive, very beguiling in what she knew was an utterly insincere way.

Yet if she was an actress, he was an even better actor.

Then as they talked together, visiting the Pump Rooms in the morning, driving during the afternoon in a Phaeton which Julius hired at a vast expense, she began to think that he did in fact find her rather attractive.

The compliments he paid her she dismissed, but on the third afternoon as they drove out into the country he began to talk about himself in a manner that he had not done before.

She felt then that perhaps for the first time he was thinking of her as a woman and not as a bank balance.

He told her how much he enjoyed London and how exciting it had been to find he could move with the Bucks and Dandies of St James' and was accepted in all the best Clubs, besides being invited to all the important houses of the *Beau Monde*.

'Have you ever been to any London parties?' he enquired.

Giselda shook her head.

'You will find them very different from those you have enjoyed in Yorkshire.'

'I am afraid I should be very much a country mouse.'

'That is untrue,' Julius answered. 'You would shine like a star, and I should be as proud of being your escort there as I am here.'

There was now a note of sincerity in his voice which made Giselda feel uncomfortable.

Although it was what the Earl and Henry Somercote had expected she shrank from the moment when Julius Lynd would propose marriage to her and she would refuse him.

She could not help feeling that however bad a man might be, however discreditable, to make him a laughing-stock and humiliate him was cruel.

For the first time since she had undertaken the part the Earl had found for her she felt ashamed of deceiving Julius.

There was no reason why she should.

She had listened to him boasting and telling her in-numerable lies during the first days of their acquaintance.

She had known that he was pursuing her entirely for her supposed money, even as he had pursued the unat-tractive ageing Miss Clutterbuck.

At the same time she still disliked the thought that she must act a lie and perpetrate a falsehood on anyone, how-ever badly they might have behaved.

Yesterday, because she had felt that Julius was growing near to a declaration of his affections, she had changed the subject, admiring the buildings of which Colonel Berkeley was so proud, and had insisted on returning earlier than Julius wished her to do.

She realised that it was easy for him to be more inti-mate in his conversation when they were driving than when they walked down the tree-lined approach to the Pump Room.

There there were plenty of 'water-drinkers' to make privacy impossible, but in a Phaeton without a groom up behind, Giselda felt very vulnerable.

Both the Earl and Henry Somercote were waiting for her on her return to German Cottage, and because she felt somewhat guilty at her part in the deception she answered their questions abruptly and as soon as she could withdrew to her own bedroom.

'What has upset her?' Henry asked the Earl when they were alone.

'I have no idea.' the Earl replied.

'Can it be possible that she is developing an affection for young Julius?'

'If anything is completely impossible, that is,' the Earl said sharply. 'On one thing I would stake my life, if necessary, that Giselda would not be taken in by that cheap philanderer.'

'I hope you are right,' Henry replied, 'but after all she is very young and, whatever you and I may think of him, Julius is quite a presentable young man.'

The Earl was scowling and after a moment he said:

'If I thought such a thing was even remotely possible I would stop this charade immediately and let Julius marry that Clutterbuck creature, whatever the consequences!'

'I do not believe you need perturb yourself,' Henry said, soothingly, surprised at the storm he had evoked. 'Giselda seems to have her head screwed on tight, and the one thing she must realise is that even if she grew fond of Julius, there would be no future for her without money and with him practically in the clutches of the Duns.'

He had however left the Earl in a state of some anxiety, and the following day when Giselda told him she was going to the Pump Room as usual with Julius Lynd, he asked searchingly:

'You are not becoming fond of that young reprobate, are you?'

'Fond?' Giselda asked in surprise.

'Henry thought it strange yesterday when you would not tell us what was said during your drive. I suppose he will be taking you out again this afternoon?'

Giselda was silent for a moment. Then she said:

'I merely felt a little .. uncomfortable at having to tell so many lies. I was brought up to think they were wicked and my Nurse believed that if you told enough of them you were certain to burn in all the fires of hell!'

The Earl laughed.

'I promise I will come and rescue you, or at least bring a cup of cold water. Is that reassuring?'

Giselda did not answer and as she finished bandaging his leg he said:

'Is that really what is worrying you?'

'How much .. longer do I have to go on .. doing this?' she asked in a low voice.

'As long as is necessary,' the Earl replied. 'But I suppose, even if you save Julius from Miss Clutterbuck, there will be others, although this may have taught him a lesson.'

'I wonder if this sort of lesson is ever enough?' Giselda asked. 'It will only make him resentful and hate you more than he does already.'

'He hates me?' the Earl questioned.

Giselda realised she had been indiscreet.

At the same time she thought it must have been obvious to the Earl how much Julius resented the fact that he was beholden to his cousin's generosity, and that he had refused him further monies the last time he had asked for them.

As she did not answer the Earl gave a laugh with no humour in it.

'I suppose I have been a fool in thinking that Julius might be grateful for what he has received from me in the past.'

'Perhaps he too thinks it is "more blessed to give than to receive",' Giselda said.

'Are you quoting my own words against me?' the Earl asked.

'I thought they were rather apt.'

He laughed in a very different way.

'You are trying to make me feel guilty,' he said. 'Well, quite frankly, you will never succeed in that. Julius has run through one fortune. He has beggared his mother, and if I gave him thousands of pounds today, tomorrow he would be asking for more.'

'Then what is the solution?'

'Quite frankly I do not know,' the Earl answered. 'This is only a maneouvre to prevent him from taking a very undesirable bride, and I cannot see further ahead than the moment when he will offer you his hand and his debts in marriage.'

After giving the Earl everything he wanted, she was just about to leave the room to change and put on her bonnet when she said:

'I forgot to tell you, His Grace the Duke of Wellington will be calling on you at three o'clock the day after tomorrow. His servant left a message.'

'The Duke?' the Earl exclaimed. 'Then he has arrived?'

'Yes, unexpectedly early,' Giselda answered. 'I am sure it will be considered an absolute disaster since the triumphal arches are not in place and I doubt if the address of welcome has actually been written.'

The Earl laughed.

'That will certainly put out the Colonel. He told me he had called several Committee meetings to plan exactly what should take place.'

'The Duke will still open the new Assembly Rooms, Giselda said.

'They certainly will not let him off that,' the Earl smiled, 'and I shall look forward to seeing him. Now you will be able to meet "the Immortal Deliverer of Europe"!'

Giselda stiffened and after a moment she said:

'You will excuse me, My Lord, but as I have already told you I have no wish to do that.'

'Are you serious?' the Earl enquired. 'I cannot believe

that anyone would not wish to meet the Duke. After all, he saved the world from Napoleon.'

'I am not questioning his military achievements,' Giselda said in a small voice, 'but I cannot and .. will not meet him .. personally.'

'But why? Why?' the Earl cried. 'You must have some sensible explanation for such a refusal.'

'I am sorry, but I cannot give you one,' Giselda answered. 'I want to make it clear that if you send for me while His Grace is here I will not come.'

She did not wait to hear the Earl's answer, she merely went from the room shutting the door quietly behind her.

The Earl was silent from sheer astonishment, then he swore softly to himself.

He could not imagine why Giselda should refuse to meet the Duke of Wellington, or why, if she had what she thought a good reason, she would not tell him what it was.

The whole thing was completely incomprehensible, and the fact that it constituted a problem for which he had no solution made him irritated to the point when he more or less sulked all through luncheon.

If Giselda was aware of the cause of his bad temper she did not admit it.

Instead she chatted about the people she had seen at the Pump Room that morning and the consternation in the town because the Duke, the Duchess, two sons and a suite of retainers had arrived before the flowers, flags and fireworks were ready.

What Giselda had said was confirmed by Henry Somercote, who arrived after she had left the house to drive with Julius and told the Earl what a furore the Duke's early arrival had caused.

'The Colonel is furious with me,' Henry said. 'But it was not my fault. The Old Man told me he was coming on the 20th. How was I to know he would change his mind and come on the 18th?'

'Fitz will get over it,' the Earl said consolingly, 'and by the way, it should keep him too busy to interfere in my affairs.'

'How has he done that?' Henry enquired.

'He taught Giselda how to play écarté last night.'

'Good God! I hope she did not lose!'

'No, she won ten guineas but it is a mistake for her to gamble when Julius at any rate would expect her to play for high stakes.'

'Of course it is,' Henry agreed. 'I cannot think why the Colonel should be so stupid. Usually he throws himself into a part wholeheartedly and never makes a mistake.'

'Well, he has made one now as far as I am concerned,' the Earl said, 'and I shall tell him so when I see him.'

'It is unlike him,' Henry said again. 'I hear he was brilliant when he acted with Grimaldi, the King of the Clowns. George Byron who was staying at Berkeley Castle at the same time told me about it.'

'Was Fitz really good?' the Earl asked incredulously.

'He was so good that according to Byron he almost stole the applause from Grimaldi.'

'I wonder Grimaldi agreed to perform with an amateur.'

'The Colonel gave him and his son £100 as remuneration, and Byron said that the whole of Cheltenham turned out to applaud them.'

'I am not surprised,' the Earl said. 'At the same time I wish Fitz would leave my play to me and not act the part of benefactor to Giselda.'

'He will be too busy while the Duke is here to do that again,' Henry said soothingly.

. . . . .

Because Giselda felt rather guilty at refusing so bluntly to meet the Duke of Wellington, she ordered a special dinner for the Earl the evening after His Grace was to call at three o'clock.

She discussed it with the Chef and chose the dishes His Lordship liked best.

He had taken to leaving the selection of menus to her, although he was extremely critical if her choice did not match his own ideas.

'Every woman should learn how to choose a good meal,' he said, and Giselda realised that this was one of the many things she had learnt since she had come to German Cottage.

She talked to the Butler who advised on the choice of claret the Earl would enjoy most, and then changed into one of the prettiest gowns which Madame Vivienne had provided for her.

It was of varying shades of blue, embroidered with diamanté and ornamented with bunches of pale pink roses.

The Earl had thought it was rather an unsophisticated style for the character of Mrs Barrowfield, but when Giselda had put it on she looked so entrancing in it that he insisted on buying it, even though she was as doubtful as he was whether it was suitable for a widow.

When Giselda returned from her drive which she deliberately prolonged she learnt from the servants that the Duke had left the Earl at six o'clock and his dinner was half after seven. She went along the corridor to his bedroom at about twenty minutes past the hour.

She had realised that he was still angry with her although they had not spoken again of the Duke's prospective visit.

She only hoped now that His Grace would have swept away the Earl's resentment and because they must have enjoyed talking over their experiences her sins of omission would have been forgotten.

She knocked perfunctorily on the bedroom door and opened it, then stared with astonishment at the empty bed.

She realised that the Earl had not recently vacated it

and a little bewildered she walked across the room to open the door into the adjacent Sitting-Room.

The Earl occupied the main bedroom in German Cottage, and it was in fact part of a suite with a Sitting-Room and another bedroom attached.

Because he had been in bed ever since she had known him, Giselda had hardly ever entered the Sitting-Room.

Now she realised it was a very attractive room with large windows looking out onto the garden behind the house and beyond there was a quite magnificent view of the Malvern Hills.

But for the moment she had eyes only for the man standing by the mantelpiece. It was the Earl and for the first time she was seeing him dressed.

'Good evening, Giselda,' he said in his deep voice as she stood looking at him apparently speechless.

'You are surprised to see me up!' he went on. 'But you could hardly expect me to receive my Commanding Officer except in my "best bib and tucker"!'

He smiled as he spoke and it drew Giselda towards him as if it was a magnet.

She had not realised that the Earl was so tall, so broad-shouldered, or that he could look so elegant and so incredibly handsome.

His frilled cravat tied in the very latest and most intricate style was a masterpiece from Batley's clever fingers, and if after his being ill for so long his coat did not fit quite as closely as it should, Giselda was not aware of it.

She was only entranced by the pale champagne hue of his pantaloons and by the Earl's eyes which were twinkling at her astonishment.

'You must forgive me,' he said, 'if I do not change again for dinner. I do not mind admitting it was quite a struggle for me to parade in all my finery after being *hors de combat* for so long.'

'It has not been too much for you?' Giselda asked in a low voice.

'You are not going to compliment me on my appearance?'

'You look .. magnificent, as I am sure you know, but I am worried in case you have done too much too soon.'

'I hoped to surprise you, and I have succeeded,' the Earl said. 'Actually Newell said I could get up as long as I did not stay out of bed for too long.'

'Would it not be best for you to have dinner there?'

'We are dining here,' the Earl said firmly, 'and I understand that you have chosen a special menu for the occasion. You must have been clairvoyante, Giselda.'

He spoke mockingly and she knew that he was well aware why she had taken so much trouble over dinner.

'Sit down,' she said hastily. 'Do not stand unless you have to. I know Mr Newell would not wish you to do that.'

The Earl obliged by seating himself in a high-backed armchair and Giselda also sat down.

'I had no idea that you intended to get up and get dressed,' she said after a moment.

'I planned it after I heard that the Duke was calling on me,' the Earl replied. 'But I have in fact been thinking of it for some days, and now my time for being an invalid is over, or nearly so.'

The thought came to Giselda's mind that in that case he would now dispense with her services. But there was no chance of saying any more for at that moment the servants entered bringing with them the dinner on big silver dishes emblazoned with the Berkeley crest.

Giselda fancied as they ate that the Earl was putting himself out to be an amusing companion and to make her laugh.

He told her stories of the war and talked of his house in Oxfordshire, and the improvements he intended to make as soon as he was well enough to go there.

'My father died when I was in Portugal,' he said. 'I came home for a short time and left an excellent Agent in charge, but there are a number of things which need doing that only I can attend to.'

'It will be exciting because it is now your own,' Giselda said.

'That is true,' the Earl admitted, 'and I suppose I have always looked forward to the day when I could live at Lynd Park and put my own ideas of farming into operation, besides making alterations to the house.'

'Does it need it?'

'I think so, but then every Earl of Lyndhurst has thought the same thing – or perhaps it was their wives who thought of it for them!'

He went on talking, but Giselda could not help wondering whom the Earl would marry.

She felt there must be a number of lovely ladies only waiting for him to offer such a position to them and that after all the years he had spent in war service he would be happy to settle in the country with a wife, his horses and his farms to occupy him.

They had nearly finished dinner before the Earl said:

'Have you any plans for this evening?'

'Mr Lynd wished me to go with him to the Assembly Rooms,' Giselda said, 'but I thought I would really .. rather go to bed.'

'The new Assembly Rooms?' the Earl asked.

'Yes, the Ball is taking place tonight.'

'You are thinking of refusing to be present on such an occasion?'

'I will .. go if you think I .. ought to, but I would rather .. stay here.'

'How can you possibly say such a thing?' the Earl enquired. 'When dinner is over, I suppose I shall have to go to bed whether I wish to or not, and because I am tired I will doubtless fall asleep. But you, Giselda, are young, you will want to dance and to see the excitement.'

'There will be such a crowd,' Giselda said nervously. '1,400 people are expected and ..'

She paused.

She wanted to say she had no wish to go with Julius Lynd, then she thought the Earl would think that an extremely affected remark.

After all, she was only a servant whom he had appointed as his Nurse and she had already incensed him by refusing to meet the Duke of Wellington.

How could she possibly explain that she did not wish to be present at an occasion when all the personages of distinction not only of Cheltenham but also from the whole County would be congregated together?

As the Earl seemed to be waiting for her to say something, Giselda finally murmured:

'Mr Lynd said he would .. call for me soon after .. nine o'clock. The Duke and Duchess are due to appear at ten.'

'Then you must certainly be ready for Julius when he arrives,' the Earl said sternly.

'I .. wish you could come with .. me,' Giselda said softly.

He looked at her searchingly, as if he was questioning whether she was speaking politely or if she really meant what she said.

'I am too old for such frivolities.'

'That is ridiculous, as you well know,' Giselda answered, 'and may I tell you it is what invalids always feel when they become convalescent.'

'Of course, you speak from experience,' the Earl said sarcastically.

'I do,' Giselda said earnestly. 'Everyone when they have been very ill feels that it is an effort to go back into everyday life. They shrink from it. They cling to the privacy and quiet that they have enjoyed in the sick-room and hesitate to take the first step back into the world outside.'

'You think that is what I am feeling?'

'I am sure you are! When you start talking about being

"old" and not wishing for "frivolities" remember it is only a sign that you are getting better.'

The Earl laughed.

'I accept your most logical conclusions, Nurse.'

'It is true .. I promise you it is true!' Giselda declared. 'In a short time now you will be longing to get away from Cheltenham, to do all the things you want to do at home; perhaps you will take on a number of important positions in the County, to make up for the fact that you have no longer a lot of soldiers to command.'

'At least I shall be free of being bullied and restrained from doing all the things I want to do.'

'Have I bullied you?' Giselda asked almost wistfully.

'Abominably!' the Earl said, but his eyes were smiling and when she looked at him to see if he was really serious he laughed.

'You have behaved exactly as a Nurse should, but I am not yet ready to dispense with your services.'

He saw a light come into her eyes and knew without being told that she had been afraid of that.

'We will talk about it tomorrow,' he said. 'As a matter of fact I do feel rather tired.'

'Of course you do,' Giselda said, 'and if you had listened to me you would have had your dinner in bed.'

'I have enjoyed the novelty of sitting at a table and of dining with a very attractive lady,' he replied.

He raised his glass as he spoke in a silent toast, then rose a little awkwardly to his feet.

'Your leg is hurting you!' Giselda said accusingly.

'A little,' he admitted, 'but it is to be expected.'

'Not if you had not been so foolhardy,' she retorted.

She moved nearer to him and put her arm round his waist so that he could rest his on her shoulders.

She could not help feeling a rather strange sensation because she was touching him so closely and their bodies were against each other's as they moved across the room to the bedroom.

Batley was waiting and as they appeared he came forward saying:

'Now come along, M'Lord, you've been up for far too long, and you'll get Miss Giselda and me in trouble with the doctor, and that's a fact!'

'Stop nagging me, Batley, and get me into bed,' the Earl replied.

There was a note in his voice that told both Batley and Giselda that he was in fact exhausted.

Giselda left him to Batley's ministrations and when a quarter of an hour later she peeped into the room he was almost asleep.

However as she went nearer to the bed he put out his hand and took hers.

'You are to go to the Reception,' he said, 'I want you to enjoy yourself, and it is an occasion you may never see again.'

'I will go .. if you want me to,' Giselda said in a low voice.

'Promise me!'

'I .. promise.'

Almost before she said the last words she knew the Earl was asleep.

Very gently she took her hand from his.

His eyes were closed, at the same time she knew as she looked at him that it was not that he looked different, but that something different had happened between them since he had left his bed.

For the first time Giselda was thinking of him, not as an invalid, but as a man.

For the first time he was not someone who needed her care and evoked her pity, but a man, handsome and masculine, and with whom she had dined on equal terms.

For some seconds she stood beside the bed, then she turned and slipped quietly away.

.   .   .   .   .   .

The new Assembly Rooms were filled to suffocation and Giselda was thankful that she had need not be ashamed of her appearance amongst the beautiful gowns and the glitter of jewels and decorations with which all the guests seemed to be adorned.

At ten o'clock exactly the Duke of Wellington accompanied by the Duchess appeared in the Rooms to be greeted with cheers and claps.

'Cousin Talbot ought to be here to introduce us,' Julius said in Giselda's ear.

She did not tell him that she had refused to meet the Duke that afternoon.

Instead she moved around the Rooms, admiring them and realising that the Colonel had not exaggerated when he said that new, better and bigger buildings were needed in Cheltenham.

She thought she must remember everything she saw so that she could describe it to the Earl.

The exterior she had thought when they arrived was austere and undistinguished, but the Ballroom was magnificent and the Duke led the dancing with his wife as his partner.

After that everyone took the floor, but having danced once with Julius, Giselda suggested that they move out of the crowd to look at the rest of the building.

They had not proceeded far when they came upon the Colonel looking exceedingly distinguished in his knee-breeches and wearing a number of glittering decorations on his satin evening-coat.

He greeted Giselda by kissing her hand, then said to Julius:

'I wonder, dear boy, if you would be kind enough to dance with Lady Dennington who is staying with me at Berkeley Castle? There is not time for me to take the floor this evening, and as she is an exquisite dancer I know you will enjoy waltzing with her.'

Before Julius could reply he introduced him to Lady

Dennington and Giselda found herself alone with the Colonel.

'I want to talk to you,' he said.

Putting his hand under her elbow he led her across a crowded Ante-room into a smaller one, which seemed to be practically deserted.

'Let us sit down for a moment,' the Colonel suggested. 'I have been on my feet since early this morning. I am glad of a rest.'

'This must have taken a great deal of arrangement,' Giselda said.

'It did, and I am proud to say that it is a success,' the Colonel answered. 'It is in fact the best advertisement that Cheltenham could possibly have.'

'I am sure it is,' Giselda agreed.

'I do not want to talk about Cheltenham at the moment,' the Colonel said, 'but about you.'

'About me?' Giselda's eyes widened.

'I have been watching you these last few days,' he said, 'and I think you are in fact a natural actress.'

Giselda stared at him wide-eyed and he went on:

'Have you thought what you will do when the Earl no longer requires your services as a Nurse?'

Giselda was still.

It was a question that had haunted her, but she had not expected her thoughts to be repeated in words by the Colonel.

'I am sure I will find .. something,' she answered.

'You will need employment?'

'Yes .. of course.'

'I thought that was the truth,' he said. 'You would hardly be working in German Cottage as a housemaid unless you were poverty-stricken.'

Giselda said nothing.

She felt it was rather cruel of him to remind her at this moment, when she hoped she was looking attractive, of her position before the Earl had rescued her.

'When the Earl leaves,' the Colonel went on, 'I have a place for you, Giselda, in the theatre.'

She looked at him incredulously.

'In the theatre?' she repeated.

'That is what I said,' he answered. 'My players are amateurs, but I recompense them liberally, and I will see that you are not without money when you are no longer performing this part.'

There was something in the way he spoke which made Giselda look at him questioningly.

As if he understood what she asked without words he said :

'You are very attractive! More attractive than I can tell you at the moment when you are still, as it were, under the protection of my friend. But I shall have a great deal to say on the matter, Giselda, as soon as you are free.'

Because suddenly Giselda understood what he was insinuating the colour rose in her cheeks.

'I . . I cannot listen . . I do not think . .' she stammered.

She was interrupted by the Colonel.

'There is no need for you to say anything,' he said. 'I realise the position in which you find yourself, and of course your loyalty for the time being is to the Earl. But my dear, you can trust me to be very kind to you, and the position I will offer you in the future would certainly not be that of maid-servant in my house.'

He bent a little nearer to her as he spoke and instinctively Giselda recoiled, then she rose to her feet.

'I think, Sir . . I should go . . home,' she said in a frightened voice.

'Leave everything to me, Giselda,' the Colonel said, and he was not speaking of her leaving the Assembly Rooms. 'Your future is assured and I shall be only waiting for the moment when we can discuss it together.'

Without answering Giselda turned away from him and moved towards the Ante-room through which they had come.

She did not know if the Colonel was following her for she did not look back.

She just walked steadily towards the Ballroom, and when she reached it she saw to her relief that the dance had ended and Julius was coming towards her, Lady Dennington leaning on his arm.

He escorted his partner to the nearest chair, and when she had seated herself he bowed and came immediately to Giselda's side.

'Of all the impertinence!' he said. 'The Colonel fobbing me off on that boring woman! She could talk of nothing but her ailments which have brought her here.'

'I would like to go home,' Giselda said.

'And I will gladly take you,' Julius replied. 'If you ask me, these social crushes are always too hot and a dead bore!'

Giselda was inclined to agree with him.

There was a long line of carriages for hire waiting outside the Assembly Rooms and it was too early in the evening for them to be in short supply.

Julius handed her into one and as they drove off he took her hand and said:

'I regret that we wasted this evening in that crush; the Colonel's behaviour is indefensible.'

'I am sure he meant it kindly,' Giselda managed to say.

In reality she agreed that the Colonel had behaved extremely badly in more ways than Julius realised.

'How dare he?' she thought. 'How dare he suggest such things to me!'

Then she remembered what she had asked the Earl to do for her when she had been desperate to find the £50 for Rupert's operation.

'Is that what I have sunk to?' she asked herself and felt ashamed and somehow unclean.

It was not a long drive to German Cottage, and although Julius was talking she found it impossible to listen to what he was saying.

Only as the horses drew up outside the door did she hear him say:

'You promise? You really promise me that?'

'What did I promise?' Giselda asked.

'You just said you would dine with me one night,' Julius answered, 'and alone.'

'Did I?'

'Of course you did, and now you cannot take back your word once you have given it. I shall hold you to that, Mrs Barrowfield! For I wish to talk to you alone, where we shall not be disturbed.'

He spoke with a passionate intensity which made Giselda feel embarrassed. Then to her relief the footmen came down the steps to open the carriage door.

'I will think about it,' she said.

'And I may call for you at ten o'clock tomorrow morning?'

'Yes, of course.'

At least, she thought, they could not be alone walking down the avenue of elm-trees to the Pump Room and waiting with a hundred other people for the glass of water to be poured by Mrs Forty.

'Then you must give me a date on which you will keep your promise,' Julius said.

Giselda did not reply and he kissed her hand. Then she was free of him, but not, she told herself as she went up the stairs, free of the Colonel and his proposition which the more she thought of it the more it shocked and horrified her.

'I hate him!' she thought. 'I hate him and I hate Julius Lynd – in fact I hate all men!'

Then as she passed the Earl's bedroom she knew that was untrue; for there was one man she did not hate – one man who did not shock or frighten her.

One man whom she wanted to tell now at this moment of what had happened.

'But that,' Giselda told herself sternly, 'is something I must never do.'

The Colonel was his friend, and not only had she no wish to be a disruptive influence between the two men who were fond of each other, but more than that, the last thing she must ever do was to accept charity from the Earl.

'I must be strong and resolute about that,' Giselda said to herself as she went into her own bedroom.

When she thought of the future without the Earl she was afraid — desperately and agonisingly afraid.

5

The sunshine came in through the open windows of the Breakfast Room and glittered blindingly on the silver coffee pot.

There was, Giselda noticed as she sat down, a new honeycomb and a pat of golden Jersey butter which came from Colonel Berkeley's farms at the Castle.

It was a thrill to realise as the Earl sat opposite her how well he looked and that even in the bright morning light the pallor on his face was much less noticeable, in fact his skin seemed quite brown against the whiteness of his cravat.

'I am actually hungry this morning,' the Earl remarked as he helped himself to veal chops cooked with fresh mushrooms.

'That is a good sign,' Giselda smiled.

'But not as hungry as I shall be when I return home,' he went on. 'There I always ride before breakfast and come in ready to do justice to the many dishes that are waiting for me.'

'You have fine horses at Lynd Park?' Giselda asked.

'Very fine,' the Earl replied, 'but I intend to buy a great many more. My father was not interested in racing, which I am, and as soon as I am well enough I intend to ride in the local steeplechases.'

There was an enthusiasm in the Earl's voice that was almost boyish, and Giselda felt a pain in her heart as she realised that while he was planning all these things in the future she would not be there.

She wondered if, when he was riding across his Park

and over his big estate, he would ever think of her, and she knew with a sudden sense of inevitability that she would never be able to forget him even for a moment.

He seemed to be ever in her thoughts and in her mind, part of her consciousness from which she could never be free, and as she envisaged a future without him she knew suddenly and unmistakably that she loved him.

She had not realised before that what she felt for him was love; in fact until he was up and dressed she had not really thought of him as a man.

But now it was impossible to think of him in any other way and she knew that he filled her whole life.

'How strange to realise at breakfast, of all times, that one is in love,' she thought to herself.

But she knew that the love that lived in her heart had been there for a long time.

It was simply that she had been afraid to acknowledge it.

'Whatever happens,' she told herself, 'he must never know .. never have the least idea that I feel like this.'

Because perhaps she was in some ways the actress the Colonel thought her to be, she managed to say in quite a normal voice:

'What plans have you for today?'

'I have not really decided,' the Earl replied.

As he spoke a footman came into the room with a letter on a silver salver.

The man walked towards the table and the Earl waited, obviously expecting the letter to be for him, but instead the footman offered it to Giselda.

'A *billet-doux*?' the Earl enquired, raising his eyebrows.

Giselda took the note from the salver.

'May I open this?' she enquired politely.

'Please do,' the Earl replied. 'I assure you that I am extremely curious!'

Giselda opened the envelope.

It was from Julius.

His writing was large, his capitals somewhat flamboyant, and she thought both characteristics were typical of his personality.

She read:

You promised to dine with me one evening and I am therefore planning a dinner which I think you will appreciate for tonight.

You can give me your answer when I take you to the Pump this morning, but it is always so difficult to speak when there are so many people around us. I want to tell you that I am looking forward more than I can ever say, to have something particular to ask you which I can only do when we are undisturbed.

Please do not disappoint your most humble and respectful admirer,

Julius Lynd

After reading the note Giselda passed it without comment to the Earl.

He read it and said briefly:

'Your answer is yes!'

'Do I .. have to .. go?'

Even as she spoke she thought what a foolish question it was.

She had been employed to inveigle Julius into making her an offer of marriage and that, she was quite certain, was what he intended to do tonight.

'Accept,' the Earl ordered.

Obediently Giselda said to the servant:

'Ask the messenger to tell Mr Lynd that I shall be very pleased to accept his invitation.'

The footman bowed and left the room and the Earl and Giselda sat silent.

The Earl helped himself to another dish and when he had done so he said:

'I will ring when we want anything else.'

'Very good, M'Lord.'

The servants left the Breakfast Room and Giselda waited.

'As you must be well aware, Giselda,' the Earl said after a moment, 'that when we began this masquerade the reason for it was two-fold, first to deter Julius from marrying Miss Clutterbuck, second to make him feel a fool and to teach him not to run after rich women.'

'Do you really think that because we .. humiliate him when he asks me to marry him it will prevent him from trying to find .. another rich wife in the future?' Giselda asked.

'Perhaps not,' the Earl reflected, 'at the same time no man likes to look an idiot and Julius, when he discovers that you are absolutely penniless, will realise what a turnip-top he has made of himself.'

'And you expect .. me to tell him?'

'No, of course not,' the Earl replied. 'If he proposes to you tonight, which he undoubtedly will, I suggest you say that he should discuss it with me or alternatively, if you prefer, with the Colonel. After all, he is supposed to be your relative.'

'No .. not the Colonel!' Giselda said sharply.

'Why did you say it like that?' the Earl asked.

'I do not .. wish the Colonel to be concerned in my .. private affairs.'

The Earl looked at her searchingly as if he was not certain this was the correct explanation. Then he said:

'Very well, I will speak to Juilius. You can make the excuse that you could not marry him unless I gave my permission. He will come to me and I will tell him exactly what I think of him.'

There was a note of satisfaction in the Earl's voice, and after a moment Giselda said hesitatingly:

'I .. know Julius has behaved .. badly .. I know he has .. taken far too much money from you. At the same time .. I am sure it does you as much .. harm as it does him to be .. vindictive.'

'Vindictive?' the Earl exclaimed. 'Is that what you think I am being?'

'N . no . . not exactly,' Giselda said. 'It is just that you are so . . strong in every way, and you have so . . much.'

'Julius had a great deal too,' the Earl replied. 'I assure you I am not "grinding down the face of the poor". Julius had a large fortune which unfortunately he inherited when he was twenty-one on his father's death.'

He paused before he went on:

'He threw it all away in the space of two years, then spent practically everything his mother owned. Do you call that particularly creditable?'

'No . . you are right . . it is just that I cannot help feeling . . sorry for anyone who is poor.'

The Earl's face softened.

'I can understand that, Giselda, it is what I would expect you to feel, but do not waste your sympathy on Julius. If you were as wealthy as he thinks you are, he would run through your fortune in a few years and then not hesitate to abandon you while he chased after other women.'

'I wonder if anyone is really all bad?' Giselda said.

'Or all good,' the Earl said cynically, 'with the exception, perhaps, of yourself.'

Giselda smiled.

'I wish that was true. I am not good. I often hate people very bitterly.'

'The Duke of Wellington, for instance.'

He saw Giselda's eyes widen and realised that on drawing his bow he had hit the bull's-eye.

'You *do* hate him?' he asked slowly. 'Is it quite useless for me to ask the reason?'

'Quite . . useless.'

'Well, let me tell you one thing,' the Earl said. 'I intend to discover your secrets however cleverly you may hide them, and one day, because I am very persistent, I shall succeed, however much you may try to stop me.'

Giselda did not answer, she just looked at him and the Earl saw an expression in her eyes that he could not explain.

It was not only fear; there was something else and while he was still wondering what it could be, the door opened and Colonel Berkeley came into the doom.

'Good morning, Giselda – good morning, Talbot!' he said. 'It is delightful to see you up and actually downstairs for breakfast!'

'It is something I am enjoying,' the Earl replied. 'You are an early caller, Fitz.'

'I have a great deal to do today,' he answered, 'and I have come to ask you to be my guest this evening.'

'Where?' the Earl enquired.

'At the play which I am putting on for the Duc d'Orléans. I expect you know that he is in Cheltenham and he has especially asked to see this new production I was telling you about.'

'*The Villain Unmasked*?' the Earl remarked with a smile.

'So you remembered!' the Colonel said with pleasure.

He pulled up a chair to the table, and as if anticipating his wish a servant set a large cup in front of him and filled it with coffee.

'It is going to be an entertaining evening with a very distinguished audience,' the Colonel said as he picked up the cup, 'and I really think it will amuse you, Talbot. Besides Maria Foote is playing the lead and I want you to see her.'

As the Earl did not reply the Colonel turned to Giselda.

'He is well enough to enjoy an evening out, is he not, Nurse?' he enquired.

He spoke jokingly but there was an expression in his eyes that made Giselda feel embarrassed and she looked only at the Earl as she replied:

'Mr Newell is very pleased with His Lordship.'

'Then you must rest this afternoon, Talbot, and come

to the theatre at eight o'clock. Afterwards, if you do not feel too tired, you must have supper with Maria and me. We will not keep you up late, and by the way I have already asked Henry Somercote to accompany you.'

'You leave me little alternative but to accept,' the Earl said slowly.

'I want you to see me in this new part,' the Colonel replied. 'Although I say it myself, I am extremely good in it!'

He drank some of his coffee and then as if he had suddenly thought of it he said:

'Another night you must bring Giselda to see me, but not tonight. As you will not wish to climb the stairs I am putting you in the Stage-Box. It holds three people, but I have to occupy one seat during the course of the play.'

'Why is that?' the Earl enquired.

'Because as the nobleman who seduces the innocent maiden I persuade her to take part in the stage in defiance of her father's wishes who is a Clergyman.'

He laughed.

'It is really rather amusing. The Clergyman spends the First Act declaiming against bloodshed of any sort and in preaching that all Christians must turn the other cheek however much they are insulted. Then at the end of Act Two, to avenge the seduction of his daughter he shoots the nobleman who was responsible while he sits in the Stage-Box of the theatre!'

'It all sounds very ingenious to me,' the Earl remarked with just a touch of sarcasm in his voice. 'Are you responsible for such "blood and thunder"?'

'It was principally written by a young protégé of mine,' the Colonel replied, 'but I must admit to having added several twists to the plot that he had not originally considered!'

The Earl laughed.

'The trouble with you, Fitz, is that you will do everything yourself. You want to be the author, the producer, the stage-manager, the principal actor, and I om only surprised you do not also conduct the orchestra!'

'My dear Talbot,' the Colonel answered, 'I have learnt in life that if one wants a thing doing well one has to do it oneself. Anyway, tonight you will see what I can do. The theatre is packed! Every seat is sold out, so please do not leave the Stage-Box empty. It would stand out like a missing tooth.'

'As my host, and since I am extremely grateful to you for bringing me to Cheltenham,' the Earl said, 'you make it impossible for me to say anything but thank you.'

'A very pretty speech,' the Colonel said mockingly, 'and now I will leave you and your very attractive Nurse to finish your breakfast.'

He rose to his feet. Then looking at Giselda he said:

'I am anticipating that one day Giselda will play a part in one of my productions, and when that happens you must certainly be in the Stage-Box.'

The Earl looked at him in astonishment, but before he could say anything the Colonel had left the room and they heard his voice speaking loudly to one of the servants in the passage outside.

'What the devil did he mean by that?' the Earl enquired.

Giselda looked embarrassed.

'The other night .. at the opening of the Assembly Rooms .. he suggested that as I had .. acted this part so .. well I might like to act for him in the .. future.'

It was difficult to say the words, especially when she realised that the Earl was looking at her searchingly.

'He said that to you?' he ejaculated. 'Why did you not tell me?'

'I . I did not think the Colonel was .. serious.'

The Earl's lips tightened.

'He is usually serious when it concerns his plays,' he said, 'and what you are really telling me is that he offered you employment when you should leave mine.'

'Y . yes.'

'Had you any idea that he might have other reasons for asking you to do this?'

There was silence and the Earl fancied that for a moment Giselda did not understand what he meant. Then the colour rose in her cheeks.

She looked away from him out into the garden.

'You suspected it at any rate,' the Earl said dryly.

'I could not .. credit that was .. what he meant,' she murmured.

'He will have meant it all right!' the Earl said. 'Let me put this bluntly, Giselda, unless you think it desirable to become one of the Colonel's many mistresses I should not listen to such a proposition.'

'No .. of course not .. I had no .. intention of doing so.'

'Then why did you not tell me about it?'

There was silence and after a moment the Earl said:

'I would like you to answer that question.'

'I thought .. you might be .. annoyed,' Giselda faltered. 'He is .. your friend .. and you were staying .. in his house.'

'You were thinking of me?'

'Yes .. I did not want you .. upset or angry .. when you were getting so much .. better in health.'

'Let me make one thing clear,' the Earl said. 'You are at the moment in my employment and there is no question of it coming to an end until the problem over Julius is finally and completely settled.'

Giselda did not answer and after a moment he said:

'You had better get ready if you are going to the Pump Room with him. We will discuss your future at a later date.'

'Yes .. My Lord .. and thank you,' Giselda said.

She rose from the table, and as if she wished to escape from the embarrassing situation she went hurriedly from the room.

The Earl threw his table-napkin down angrily on the table as if the mere action gave him some relief from the feelings inside him. Then he walked out into the garden, moving slowly over the green lawn.

·   ·   ·   ·

There was the usual crowd at the Pump Room and there had been so many people walking along the tree-lined walk towards it that Giselda realised with a sense of relief that it was impossible for Julius to say anything intimate.

She had felt ever since breakfast as if her breathing was constricted and there was something hard and uncomfortable within her breasts.

She could not bear to think that the Earl should imagine for one moment that she had seriously considered the Colonel's invitation.

Yet it had been impossible to tell him so or to put into words how shocked and indeed disgusted she had been by his suggestions.

All she could think of now was that the Earl was angry with her and she felt as if she was encompassed by a fog rather than the sunshine.

Every word that she had to say to Julius was an effort because it brought her thoughts away from the Earl and back to him.

The Montpellier Pump Room was not impressive. It was a long, unpretentious building with wooden pillars, a verandah and a small structure over the centre for an orchestra.

This was filled with a number of players who provided soft music while the drinkers approached the Pump and having received their glasses of water stood about gossiping while they drank it.

Julius fetched Giselda a glass and as he gave it into her hand said in a low voice:

'You look so lovely, Mrs Barrowfield, that no one

would believe for a moment that you needed medicinal waters.'

Because she felt shy at the note in his voice Giselda said quickly:

'It seems strange to think that all these people should be here just because of some pigeons.'

'Pigeons?' Julius enquired in surprise.

'Have you not heard the legend?' Giselda asked. 'The properties of the well were discovered about a hundred years ago when it was noticed that the pigeons flocked to peck at the deposits of salt here.'

Julius did not look particularly interested but because Giselda wished to keep talking she said:

'It was found that the water was rich in natural salts and the people of Cheltenham, realising that other Spas like Bath and Tonbridge were flourishing, saw to it that the rumours of their waters were soon spread.'

'It has certainly brought the town a lot of money,' Julius remarked.

His tone was envious and Giselda thought with a little sigh that it was difficult for him to think of anything else but his financial burdens.

Because she was afraid that he might become intimate she looked around and, seeing a distinguished-looking man with a small imperial beard and a large pointed moustache, she asked:

'Is that the Duc d'Orléans?'

Julius looked in the direction of her eyes and nodded.

'Yes, it is.'

'I heard he was here. He is going to the theatre tonight to see the Colonel's play.'

'How did you know that?' Julius enquired.

'The Colonel arrived while we were at breakfast,' Giselda explained, 'and invited His Lordship to sit in the Stage-Box with Captain Somercote.'

She smiled before she continued:

'It will be rather exciting for them because they will

be almost part of the play. The Colonel joins them at the end of the Second Act and is shot by one of the actors on the stage.'

'You cannot go with them – you are dining with me,' Julius said almost fiercely.

'Yes, of course. I have not forgotten that, and actually the Colonel did not include me in his invitation. There would not be room for me in the Box.'

'Even if he had done so I should have held you to your promise.'

'Which I should not have broken,' Giselda said.

She saw the gladness in Julius's face and thought she was not mistaken in thinking that, even if he was going to ask her to marry him for her money, he also had a slight, even if it was very slight, affection for her.

She was just about to hand him her glass saying she had finished her water, which she was quite convinced was nastier every time she drank it, when unexpectedly there was a woman standing beside Julius.

'I want to speak to you, Mr Lynd.'

The woman spoke abruptly, but there was something in the tone of her voice which commanded attention, and Julius turning to face her gave a noticeable start.

'I want to tell you,' the woman went on, 'that I am leaving Cheltenham this afternoon.'

It was then that Giselda guessed who she was.

There was no mistaking that the woman was extremely unprepossessing and getting on in middle age, and she was certain that she was Emily Clutterbuck.

She was in fact positively ugly, and yet because of that very ugliness Giselda could not help thinking there was something pathetic about her.

She was expensively dressed although her gown was not in good taste; her bonnet sported too many green ostrich feathers; and the jewels round her neck and on her wrists were valuable but ostentatious.

Giselda could not help noticing that the cosmetics with which she tried to hide the roughness of her skin were not skilfully applied.

Perhaps because she was agitated, the salve on her lips was smudged and it was easy to realise she was in fact very nervous.

'If you are leaving this afternoon, then I must wish you good-bye and God-speed,' Julius said.

He had recovered from the start he had given at the sight of Miss Clutterbuck and from seeming for the moment tongue-tied.

'There is something I want to say to you.'

Julius glanced uncomfortably at Giselda but there was nothing he could do to prevent Emily Clutterbuck from continuing:

'When I came here,' she said, 'you had raised my hopes in a – manner which I now realise was only part of my – imagination and yet because you made me feel for a short time at any rate – that I was a woman – like other women – I want to thank you.'

'T . to t . thank m . me?' Julius stammered.

There was no doubt now that he was acutely embarrassed.

'Yes, to thank you,' Emily Clutterbuck said. 'I have not had much happiness in my life, but this last month I have been happy. Although I know it was foolish of me to expect – any more, I shall at least have some – memories – memories of you, Mr Lynd, and all the – wonderful things you said to me.'

There was an unmistakable sob as she spoke the last words. Then bending her head with its tasteless array of ostrich feathers she turned and walked away.

For a moment Julius stared after her in a bemused fashion, then turned to Giselda to say in a loud, blustering voice:

'Well, really! I cannot imagine anyone could be so insensitive, so . .'

Giselda put out her hand and dug her fingers into his arm.

'Go after her,' she said insistently. 'Go after her and say something nice. Give her something to remember. Be kind .. be really kind. It will not hurt you .. but it will mean .. everything to that poor .. woman.'

For a moment she thought he would defy her and refuse to do as she asked.

Then as her eyes met his and he saw how much in earnest she was, he turned on his heel and strode after Emily Clutterbuck who by this time was some way down the long walk.

Giselda saw them standing talking together in the shade of the overhanging trees. Then, as if she felt it was something too private to look at, she took her glass back to the counter.

She realised as she put it down that her hand was shaking and she knew that she was not only moved by the pathos of Emily Clutterbuck, but also that she hated Julius with a violence that surprised her.

She not only hated but despised him.

How could a man – any man – behave as he had behaved to that poor, ugly creature who could not help looking the way she did, but still had feelings and emotions just like any other women?

Giselda could imagine how Julius, handsome and elegant and coming from such a noble family, had seemed, when he appeared in her life, like a meteor flashing across the sky.

Of course she had come to Cheltenham hoping that the protestations of interest and affection he had made to her would be translated into a tangible proposal of marriage.

She would have thought of him all day, Giselda told herself, and dreamt of him at night.

She was certain without being told that Emily Clutterbuck would never before have met a gentleman of Julius's standing.

There was no doubt, if one did not compare him with the Earl or indeed for that matter with Henry Somercote or the Colonel, he was definitely prepossessing.

Then suddenly, like a blind being drawn over a window, he had ignored her and concentrated, as the Earl had intended him to do, on a richer and definitely better-looking heiress.

'How could anyone be so despicable?' Giselda asked herself.

Then she thought that her part in the drama was almost as reprehensible.

Julius had pretended an affection he did not feel for Emily Clutterbuck; but she was pretending to be someone she was not, merely to receive him and because the Earl wished to prevent his marriage to that poor, unhappy creature.

It was useless for Giselda to tell herself that the suffering Emily Clutterbuck would have endured once she was married to Julius would have exceeded anything she was feeling at this moment.

She knew only too well that love was not always the happy, ecstatic state that novelists depicted.

It was pain, it was misery, it was a yearning for the unattainable which she was feeling now. In her mind she linked herself with Emily and knew that they both felt the same.

They both loved a man who was out of reach. They both looked towards a future that was dark and empty without light or hope.

Giselda was so intent on her thoughts that Julius startled her when she heard his voice and realised that he was beside her again.

'I did as you asked me.'

There was a sulky note in his voice which told her it had been an uncomfortable moment.

'Thank you.'

They automatically began to walk back from the Pump

Room. 'Will you come driving with me this afternoon?'

'I am afraid that is impossible,' Giselda replied. 'I have some books to change for His Lordship, and various other things to do.'

'He will be resting if he intends to go to the theatre tonight.'

'He may wish me to read to him.'

Giselda spoke without thinking and it was quite a shock when Julius said:

'I really do not see why you should do all these things for my cousin. After all, he has a mass of servants in attendance.'

She had forgotten for the moment that she was the rich Mrs Barrowfield who need wait on no one, and now to gloss over the fact that she had made a mistake she said quickly:

'I assure you I am only too willing to be of assistance. After all, the Earl received his wounds in battle, and none of us can do too much for the men who fought for us against the tyranny of Napoleon Bonaparte.'

Julius merely looked more sulky and she knew it was because he himself had not gone to war.

'Besides,' Giselda said, elaborating. 'I wish to go to Williams' Library and try the weighing-machine. I hope to have put on a little weight during my stay at Cheltenham and I think I may have succeeded. Anyway, I shall know it for a fact after I have been there this afternoon.'

'But you will dine with me tonight?'

'Of course. I am . . looking forward to it.'

It was an effort to say the words and yet Giselda made herself say them.

How could she let down the Earl by showing Julius all too clearly as she wished to do what she really thought of him?

As if he felt some explanation was necessary he said after a moment:

'I had once some business with Miss Clutterbuck's

father, that is how we met. Of course women of that class misinterpret ordinary politeness as something very different.'

Giselda felt herself freeze.

If she had hated him before she hated him even more at this moment.

How dare he refer to Emily Clutterbuck as 'a woman of that class' when, if it had not been for the Earl's intervention, they would doubtless at this moment be announcing their engagement?

'I am afraid the lady in question seems very .. unhappy,' she said after a moment.

'I am sure she will soon get over it,' Julius said lightly, 'and I assure you, if she is, it is not my fault,'

The words she longed to say trembled on Giselda's tongue. Then she was thankful they had reached the end of the walk and Julius's Phaeton was waiting for them.

'Is there anywhere I can take you before you return to German Cottage?' he asked.

'No, thank you.'

She felt she could not bear the proximity of him any longer and they drove in silence until on reaching the Cottage, Julius drove the horses up the short drive with an almost theatrical flourish.

'Shall I call for you this evening?' he asked.

'I am sure I can arrange for one of the Colonel's carriages to convey me to The Plough,' Giselda answered. 'It is only a very short distance.'

'Then I will be waiting eagerly until you arrive – very, very eagerly!'

He raised her fingers to his lips and she had the greatest difficulty in not snatching them away.

She walked into the house and went into the Sitting-Room without taking off her bonnet or shawl.

The Earl, as she expected, was seated on the terrace just outside the French windows reading a newspaper.

She walked towards him feeling as if she needed the comfort of his presence, and some part of her noted automatically how handsome he looked and how much at his ease.

He looked up at her approach but did not rise, and she walked to stand beside his chair thankful to be with him, and yet finding it impossible for the moment to find an excuse.

'What has upset you?' he asked after a moment.

'Is it so . . obvious?' Giselda enquired.

'It is to me,' he replied. 'Sit down and tell me what has happened.'

'It is . . Mr Lynd.'

'I presume he has offered you marriage.'

'No . . it is not that.'

'Then what is it?'

'We went to the Well,' Giselda explained, 'and while we were there Miss Clutterbuck came up to him to say good-bye.'

'And that upset you?'

'She was so unhappy . . and yet . . so brave.'

Giselda drew in her breath.

'She thanked Mr Lynd for making her, for a very short time . . feel like other . . women.'

There was no mistaking the note in Giselda's voice.

She seated herself on a chair beside the Earl, and now she looked away across the garden trying to prevent the tears from coming into her eyes.

'I warned you that Julius was a young swine!' the Earl said.

'It would not have mattered so much if she were not so very . . ugly,' Giselda said.

The Earl did not speak and after a moment she went on:

'It is cruel and wrong that we should judge people by their external appearance when inside they feel the same

132

emotions as everybody else, and suffer perhaps even more acutely.'

'It is impossible for men and women to be equal,' the Earl said quietly, 'except of course in the sight of God.'

'I cannot help feeling that is very little consolation in this world,' Giselda replied.

The Earl picked up a small silver bell which stood on the table beside him and rang it.

'I am going to give you a drink,' he said, 'and something more palatable than the water you have been drinking. This has upset you, Giselda, and I understand and respect you for it. At the same time I have no wish for Julius's behaviour to add to your own troubles.'

'I cannot . . help it . . can I ?' Giselda said.

A servant appeared and the Earl gave him an order and when they were alone again he said :

'Forget Miss Clutterbuck, forget Julius for that matter ! It is useless to waste your thoughts on him.'

'This morning I told you not to be bitter about him,' Giselda said in a low voice. 'I thought it might hurt . . you . . but now I . . hate him ! I hate him in a way which I know is . . wrong !'

'Forget him !' the Earl said briefly. 'Take off your bonnet, Giselda and enjoy the sunshine.'

She obeyed him, putting her bonnet down on an adjacent chair and raising her hands to tidy her hair.

'It looks very lovely,' the Earl said, 'and quite different from the way it appeared when I first saw you without that disfiguring mob-cap.'

She looked at him in surprise and he went on :

'Your hair was starving like your body. Now it is shining with new lights and there is a buoyancy about it which was not there before.'

'I noticed it . . but I am surprised that . . you should have done so.'

'I notice everything about you, Giselda.'

Giselda felt a little tremor of warmth run through her

at his words, then the servant appeared with an ice-bucket containing a bottle of champagne.

As it was being opened Giselda told herself that the Earl was speaking impersonally. He was just producing her for a part as the Colonel produced his actors on the stage.

It amused him, because he was ill and had nothing to do, to invent a character like Mrs Barrowfield from Yorkshire, to deck her out in smart clothes, to teach her the lines she must say, and watch the reactions of the other players.

'That is all I mean to him,' she told herself.

And yet, while to feel that was true was a depressing thought, she could not help feeling excited because she was beside him and because he was prepared to listen to what she had to say.

When he handed her a glass of champagne her fingers touched his for a moment and she felt a little thrill run through her almost like quicksilver.

'I love him!' she told herself. 'I love him completely, with my heart, my mind and my very soul. He is everything I dreamt a man should be! Even if I never see him again, he will always be there in my heart.'

'This is excellent champagne,' the Earl was saying. 'Drink a little more, Giselda, it will do you good.'

Obediently Giselda, who had put down her glass after a few sips, took it up again.

'Champagne is like the happiness I feel at this moment,' she told herself, 'effervescent, but something which will not last! Yet for the moment it makes everything seem golden and glorious, as if there are no shadows waiting for me in the future.'

.   .   .   .   .

Giselda dressed early for dinner because she wished to see the Earl before he left for the theatre.

She was however so early that she went downstairs before seven o'clock to find the Earl in the Salon having a glass of wine and waiting for Henry Somercote.

They were to dine at the Cottage and the carriage was ordered for them at a quarter to seven.

Giselda entered the room conscious that she was wearing yet another new gown and hoping that the Earl would approve of it.

It was of rose-pink tulle with little touches of silver and diamanté-like dew-drops glistening in the pink magnolias which clustered in the lace around the hem and in the bodice.

But as she walked towards the Earl she was conscious not of herself and her own appearance, but of his.

She had never seen him before in full evening dress, and now she wondered if it would be possible for any man to look more impressive or more magnificent.

His black satin knee-breeches and his closely fitting long-tailed coat became him even better than anything else she had seen him wear.

His cravat was a masterpiece, and although on other occasions she had never seen him wear jewellery tonight he had a gold and emerald fob hanging beneath his satin waistcoat.

'Very pretty!' the Earl approved as she drew near to him. 'Madame Vivienne is a genius – there is no doubt about that – and this gown becomes you better than anything else I have seen you wear!'

Giselda's eyes lit up.

'I am glad you approve, My Lord.'

'If it does not bring Julius to the point – nothing will!' the Earl said abruptly, and almost, Giselda thought, unpleasantly.

'I wish I did not have to go to dine with him,' she said without thinking.

'Perhaps this is the last occasion when you will have to endure his company.'

'I hope so.'

'I have decided that Henry and I can drop you at The Plough on our way to the theatre,' the Earl said. 'I do not like to think of your travelling alone even such a short distance.'

'Thank you . . that would be very kind,' Giselda said.

Even a few minutes more with the Earl meant more than she could say.

She had been thinking this afternoon that every passing hour that she could be with him was precious.

She had the feeling that the sands were running out and soon, perhaps sooner that she dared to anticipate, he would have left Cheltenham for Lynd Park and she would no longer be able to see him.

'Will you have a glass of madeira?' he asked and she had to force her thoughts back to the commonplace.

'No thank you,' she answered, 'I think I have had enough to drink, and doubtless Mr Lynd will have ordered wine for dinner.'

'I doubt if he can order a good meal, only an expensive one,' the Earl said disagreeably. 'Fools always imagine that because a dish costs a lot of money it must be good. You and I, Giselda, know better.'

'You have taught me so much since I have been here,' she said. 'I always appreciated good food, but I did not understand the subtleties of sauces, or the flavours which come from food being cooked properly and chosen correctly in the first place.'

'There are still many things I would like to teach you,' the Earl said.

She raised her eyes to his, wanting to say that there was so much she wanted to learn, then found the words died on her lips.

There was an expression on the Earl's face which she dared not translate to herself.

Yet it set her heart beating violently and made her feel

as if something warm and wonderful moved up into her throat and strangled her very words.

They stood staring at each other. Then as if it was happening very far away they heard the door open and Henry Somercote come into the room.

·   ·   ·   ·   ·

The Earl and Captain Somercote dropped Giselda at The Plough just before seven o'clock.

She had sat talking to them while they ate their dinner and Henry Somercote had made her laugh at his stories of how the Duke had kept him running errands all day and how much the great man enjoyed finding work for other hands to do.

The Plough had a frontage of over one hundred feet on to the High Street and had, the Earl informed Giselda, the most spacious yard of any Inn in the town.

'It has stabling for a hundred horses,' he said, 'and a number of coach-houses over which there are dovecotes, besides granaries.'

Giselda learnt there were large rooms in the Inn which were let out for parties and dances, and it was where the Colonel held his committee meetings.

But the ceilings were low and there was a cosiness about the narrow passages and the small dark staircases which she found fascinating.

She was rather surprised that Julius was not waiting in the hall when she arrived. But she was immediately led upstairs.

The servant who preceded her opened a door to announce:

'The lady you were expecting, Sir.'

Giselda noticed as she entered the room that there was a table laid in the centre of it, but as Julius came forward to greet her she realised that he was not alone.

As he kissed her hand she saw that he was in evening

clothes but his appearance, while smart, did not compare with that of the Earl.

'It is because he is self-conscious about his clothes,' Giselda told herself, 'whilst the Earl makes them a part of himself and once he is dressed, does not fuss about his appearance.'

It was just a passing thought and she turned her face towards the other occupant of the room.

'I have a surprise for you,' Julius said. 'We are not to be alone this evening for the simple reason that Mr Septimus Blackett insists on playing Chaperon.'

Julius's expression was unpleasant and his voice was rude and slurred. Giselda realised that he had been drinking.

She noticed although she had not done so on arrival that his face was flushed and in fact his lips when he kissed her hand had been hot, moist and unpleasant.

Now she looked at Mr Blackett and saw that he was not in evening clothes but was dressed as might befit a clerk or even, she thought, a Commercial Traveller.

'Mr Blackett, in case you have never seen the species before,' Julius was saying in an offensive tone, 'is what, my dear Giselda, is known as a Dun. He has travelled all the way from London — think of the discomfort — to inform me that either I meet his bills which amount to a quite astronomical sum, or else I shall undoubtedly travel back to London with him at His Majesty's pleasure!'

For the moment Giselda could think of no reply. Mr Blackett, a thick-set man of perhaps forty years of age, bowed to her somewhat awkwardly.

'P . perhaps you would .. like me to .. withdraw?' Giselda managed to say at length.

'No, of course not,' Julius answered. 'There is no necessity for that. I have already explained to Mr Blackett that I shall be able to pay my bills easily and without any trouble before this evening is out, but he does not believe me and so I am afraid, Mrs Barrowfield, we shall have to put up with his quite obnoxious presence while we eat our dinner.'

Giselda took a step backwards.

'I think .. Mr Lynd .. it would be .. better for me to .. return to German Cottage. Would you be .. kind enough to order me a carriage? His Lordship and Captain Somercote brought me here and they have gone on to the theatre.'

'You must not leave me!' Julius exclaimed. 'I have planned our dinner together and not a hundred, or indeed a thousand Blacketts shall prevent us from enjoying it.'

He picked up a glass of wine he must have put down when he greeted her and drained it before he added:

'Besides, the surprise I have for Mr Blackett is one you too will enjoy. Later when we are alone together I can talk to you as I intended to do this evening.'

Giselda looked from one man to the other in perplexity.

If only the Earl was here, she thought, he would know what she should do, but he was at the theatre and it would be at least two hours before he was back at German Cottage again.

She felt helplessly that if she insisted on asking for a carriage Julius would make a scene.

He was pouring himself another glass of wine and she realised that he was already so drunk that he had forgotten to offer her a drink.

With an effort she said to Mr Blackett:

'Were the roads very bad as you came from London?'

'No, Madam, they're better at this time of the year than at any other time, and I'm glad to say very much better than they've been in the past.'

'I have known them to be almost impassable in this part of the world,' Giselda said.

'That's true, and I've had some very unpleasant journeys,' Mr Blackett replied.

They were both making an effort to behave like civilised human beings, but Julius, after pouring the wine down his throat said:

'All your journeys, Blackett, are unpleasant for someone. That is your speciality, is it not?'

There was no reply and he tugged violently at the bellpull.

'Let us have dinner. Blackett thinks it is going to be the last decent meal I shall have for a long time, but the laugh is on him! Tomorrow he is going back to London with his tail between his legs.'

'I assure you, Mr Lynd, I would rather have your money than your company,' Mr Blackett said as if he had been goaded into a response.

'That is exactly what you will have!' Julius replied: 'My money!'

Giselda tried to think what this could possibly mean. Did he really imagine that if he proposed marriage to her, which she was quite certain he intended to do, she would immediately pay his debts?

Surely no man could expect such a response from a woman, even if she was as much in love as poor Emily Clutterbuck?

Then what could be the explanation?

All through dinner she found herself becoming more and more bewildered and finding no answer to her questions.

The meal was well served and not unappetising. It was English fare at its best, and while Julius ate little and ordered bottle after bottle of wine and Giselda because she felt so agitated could only pick at her food, Mr Blackett ate heartily.

He was apparently quite unconcerned by Julius's rudeness or the way he gibed at him continually throughout the meal.

But it was very uncomfortable and Giselda longed to get away, to escape to sanity.

But course succeeded course and she realised that Julius, when he ordered dinner, had been intent on impressing her.

Finally, when it seemed as if even Mr Blackett could eat no more, dessert was put on the table, coffee was brought round and yet Giselda felt almost despairingly that it was not much after nine o'clock.

'As soon as I have finished the coffee,' she planned, 'I will leave.'

She looked at Julius as she thought it and came to the conclusion that now it would be impossible for him to prevent her.

He was sunk low on the table. The servants had put a decanter of brandy in front of him and his hand went out continually to pour himself glass after glass.

She began to wonder if anyone could drink so much and not fall insensible.

She had heard about gentlemen who collapsed under the table after dinner, but she had never actually seen anyone do it.

But now, she thought, it was only a question of time before Julius was unconscious.

She had given up making any effort to talk but while Julius had been more or less silent at the beginning of the meal he had now reached the noisy stage.

In a loud, almost incoherent voice he delivered a long harangue against the iniquities of debt collecting and in particular those scurrilous people who forced gentlemen into prisons when they could not meet their obligations.

'That is where you want to see me, Blackett,' he said, 'and that, old boy, is where you are going to be disappointed!'

He took another drink.

'In a few hours you'll be grovelling in front of me, rubbing your hands obsequiously and asking me on behalf of your clients to continue to give my patronage to your cursed inferior shops.'

He brought his fist down suddenly on the table making the glasses and cutlery rattle.

'And that is where you will make a great mistake! I am damned if I will enter any of your stinking premises again, and then you will learn what fools you have made of yourselves.'

'How can you pay the money you owe, Mr Lynd?' Giselda asked.

She felt as if it was a question which might have nasty repercussions on herself.

At the same time she was determined that now dinner was finished she would leave the room and ask one of the servants downstairs to fetch her a hackney carriage.

'That is a good question, Mrs Barrowfield, a very good question!' Julius replied. 'You are a clever woman – I have always thought that, but I am not going to answer you – yet. No, not yet. I think we have another few minutes to go.'

'Another few minutes?' Giselda questioned in bewilderment.

'Another few minutes,' Julius said with a drunken leer, 'and then you will see before you not poor Julius Lynd, not a wretched debtor with empty pockets, but – who do you think will be here?'

'I have no idea,' Giselda answered. 'Who will be?'

'The fifth Earl of Lyndhurst – that is who I will be! The fifth Earl – do you hear that, Blackett? Now you know why you will go back to London alone.'

Giselda was very still.

'What do you mean? How is that possible?' she asked.

Julius pointed an unsteady finger towards the clock.

'Bang – bang!' he said. 'Just one little bang – and the fourth Earl falls dead! Quite dead.'

Giselda started to her feet.

She moved so violently that her chair fell over backwards and crashed to the floor.

Then she pulled open the door of the private room and ran down the dark stairs.

She ran past several astonished servants, rushed through the front door and out onto the street.

Then lifting her gown with both hands she ran faster than she had ever run in her life before.

6

The carriage, having dropped Giselda at The Plough, carried the Earl and Captain Somercote up the High Street towards the Theatre Royal.

The history of Cheltenham's theatrical prowess was a remarkable one.

Originally a very small malt-house had been converted into a primitive theatre.

It was here that the young Sarah Siddons appeared in *Venice Preserved* and she moved the members of the audience so emotionally that her performance was reported to David Garrick.

Shortly afterwards she began her famous career on the London stage.

Many other great actors such as Charles Kemble, Dorothy Jordan and Harriet Mellon had played in the converted malt-house where the 'tiring-room' was a hayloft.

The Theatre Royal, although small, was elegant and airy and the architecture and colouring were only exceeded by the blaze of splendour which adorned Drury Lane.

There were two rows of boxes, one in the form of a Gallery behind which in the most ingenious manner was erected another Gallery for the servants.

The seats here only cost one shilling and sixpence, while the price for boxes was five shillings.

The Earl did not enter the theatre by the main door but by a private entrance used by Colonel Berkeley which led almost directly into the Stage-Box.

The auditorium was already filled and as he seated himself is the centre of the box with Henry Somercote at his right, leaving a seat for the Colonel to occupy later, he looked around and saw a number of people he knew.

Sitting in what was known as the 'Royal Box' was the Duc d'Orléans with two extremely attractive ladies, one of whom waved excitedly to the Earl, and in other boxes there was a flutter of handkerchiefs or fans and red lips parted with a smile, for this was the Earl's first appearance in public since he was wounded.

He bowed an acknowledgement to their greetings, then opening his programme settled down to discover who the players were besides the Colonel himself.

As the Colonel had told him, the part of the heroine was to be played by Maria Foote.

'She is not really much of an actress,' Henry Somercote said, knowing what the Earl was thinking, 'but she is exceedingly popular on account of her dancing. I am quite certain that we shall have plenty of that in the play.'

As soon as the curtain rose and Maria Foote appeared the Earl could understand why the Colonel was infatuated with her.

Of medium height, her oval face, light brown hair and lissom figure made her one of the most attractive women he had ever seen on the stage.

She had too a charming voice, and if her acting ability would never equal that of Sarah Siddons she at least looked the part of the innocent girl who was seduced by the dashing Rake played by the Colonel.

The Earl found the First Act extremely amusing, while Maria's stage father as a Parson declaimed in stentorian tones against the wickedness of men who indulged in duels and who took their revenge in violence on their fellow creatures.

When the curtain fell there was tumultuous applause from the packed theatre and the Earl leaning back in his chair remarked:

'The Colonel obviously has a success on his hands.'

'If you ask me,' Henry replied, 'the audience are equally amused by the drama they suspect is taking place off stage. I understand one of the Colonel's other *chères amies* is making extremely vocal protests against his new obsession with Maria.'

'Only the Colonel could contrive to keep so many women in play simultaneously like a juggler,' the Earl remarked.

They both laughed. Then the Box was invaded by the Earl's friends, most of them extremely beautiful women who told him eloquently with their eyes, as well as with their lips, how pleased they were to see him again.

'Now you are well we must be together,' was the message they conveyed to him one way or another.

When there was banging to notify the audience they should return to their seats the Earl remarked in an aside to his friend:

'I think it will soon be time for me to leave Cheltenham.'

Henry grinned.

He knew only too well how the Earl managed to prove elusive even to the most ardent of the 'Fair Amazons' who hunted him.

The Second Act was more emotional.

Maria as the innocent maiden was seduced by her villainous lover and then because he would not provide for her was forced to earn her living as a dancer in the theatre.

She kept her guilty secret from her father until, as the Act drew towards the end he discovered her perfidy and the fact that she had been seduced.

It was then as he stormed on to the stage during a performance he started to declaim against the wickedness of the man who had started her on the road to Hell.

As he did so the Box door opened and the Colonel came in to sit down in the empty seat.

He was looking very resplendent in the colourful embroidered full-skirted coat of the early eighteenth century.

The white wig became his somewhat sardonic features
and the glitter of diamonds in the lace at his throat made
it easy to understand why any maiden would find it hard
to refuse his blandishments.

On the stage Maria Foote knelt and wept as her father
cursed her for losing her purity and her hope of reaching
Heaven.

'As for your paramour,' he said, 'he shall not escape
my vengeance, for such creatures as he are not fit to
live!'

He turned round as he spoke, drawing a pistol from the
pocket of his long black coat.

The attention of the audience was on the Colonel as
he sat in the Stage-Box and the aggrieved father, pointing
his pistol at him, cried:

'I will kill you, for it is not right that you should continue to soil the earth with your wickedness, and destroy
the purity of the innocent. Die then, and may God have
mercy on your black soul!'

He gesticulated with the pistol towards the Stage-Box,
but strangely enough it was not pointed at the Colonel
but at the Earl.

'Die, Villain!' the actor cried, 'die, and may you rot in
the Hell from which you came!'

At the last word he should have pulled the trigger, but
even as his finger tightened the door of the Stage-Box was
flung open and a woman flung herself forward to stand in
front of the Earl with her arms outstretched.

It took the actor by surprise and although it was too
late to withdraw his finger from the trigger, the pistol
jerked as he pressed it.

The explosion was followed by a bang as the bullet hit
the gilded angel which surmounted the centre of the Box
and poured a shower of plaster onto the heads of those
beneath it.

There was a startled silence in the audience. Then the Colonel rose to his feet.

'Good God! That pistol was loaded with a real bullet!' he exclaimed.

His voice rang out and for a moment there was no reply. Then the actor, his face pale as death, replied:

'I had no idea of it – I swear I had no idea. I was told it was just a wager – a jest between two gentlemen.'

'You would have killed him!' the Colonel roared.

Now the whole audience was rising to their feet shouting and pointing at the Box.

Giselda's arms dropped to her sides and she felt the Earl's arms go round her.

She laid her head against his shoulder, fighting for breath.

She was gasping like a man who is drowning and goes down for the third time, her heart felt as if it would burst.

As the Earl held her close against him, he said urgently to Henry Somercote:

'Find Julius and get him out of England immediately! I will give him £1,000 a year so long as he does not set foot on these shores again. If he returns he will be charged with attempted murder!'

Henry Somercote with the quickness of a man used to receiving and obeying orders turned and went from the Box without a word.

Now the Colonel was yelling at the actor on the stage, and the actor was screaming back, their voices almost lost in the uproar of the audience who were all shouting advice or exclaiming at the danger that was passed.

Without even looking into the auditorium the Earl drew Giselda out of the Box and down the short passage towards the side-door.

She managed to walk although she was still finding it hard to get her breath and might have fallen to the ground if his arms had not supported her.

Outside in the street the Earl's carriage was waiting,

although the servants, not expecting their master to leave so early, were lounging comfortably on the box.

But as soon as they saw the Earl they became alert, and a footman opened the carriage door and helped Giselda inside.

The Earl followed her, moving a little stiffly because of his leg.

As the door closed he put his arms round her again and drew her against him.

'You saved my life, Giselda!' he said. 'How did you learn that Julius intended to have me shot?'

It was some seconds before Giselda could answer him. Then she gasped:

'He . he .. boasted that by .. half after nine .. he would be the .. Fifth Earl of .. Lyndhurst.'

She gave a little cry which seemed to come from her very heart, and whispered:

'I .. thought I would be .. too late .. and that you would .. die.'

'Thanks entirely to you I am alive,' the Earl said.

She had hidden her face against him and he could feel her tremble.

It was only a short distance to German Cottage and they drove in silence, Giselda gradually finding it easier to breathe and the Earl still holding her in his arms.

Only when the horses drew up outside the Cottage did he relinquish her and she stepped out while the footmen helped him to alight.

In the Hall there was a rush-backed armchair, seated in which the Earl was carried up the stairs by three footmen to his own Sitting-Room.

It was the Colonel who had suggested that it was quite needless for the Earl to exhaust himself by climbing up the stairs, even if he found it easy to descend them.

By the time Giselda reached the Sitting-Room, moving slowly from sheer exhaustion the Earl had completed his

ascent and was already filling two glasses on a side-table with champagne.

'You wish for supper, M'Lord?' the Butler asked.

'Not at the moment,' the Earl replied. 'I will ring if I require anything later.'

'Very good, M'Lord.'

The servants left the room and the Earl, having taken a sip of the glass of champagne, set it down on the table and turned towards Giselda.

'I think we are both in need of a drink . . .' he began – then stopped.

She was standing looking at him, her eyes very wide in her pale face and there was an expression in them which made the Earl hold out his arms.

She ran towards him like a child who seeks comfort and security. As he drew her close he realised she was still trembling but not now with the effort of breathing.

'It is all right, my darling!' he said tenderly. 'It is all over. There is no more danger. We shall neither of us ever see Julius again.'

'I was so . . afraid,' Giselda whispered, 'so desperately . . terribly afraid.'

There was a throb in her voice which could not be misunderstood, and very gently the Earl put his fingers under her chin and turned her face up to his.

'Why did you want to save my life?' he asked.

There was no need for Giselda to reply.

He could see the answer in her eyes and the softness of her lips, and feel it in the manner in which her whole body quivered against his like a bird in the hands of its captor.

For a long moment the Earl looked down into her eyes, then he said quietly:

'I love you, my precious!'

Giselda was still. Then as his lips found hers she gave a little sob, her body seemed to melt against him and her mouth surrendered itself to his.

The Earl thought he had never known anything so sweet, so innocent and so pure. Then as he felt Giselda respond to his kiss he drew her closer and his lips became more demanding and more insistent.

Finally when he raised his head he said in a voice that was curiously unsteady :

'I love you, my beautiful one! I love you more than I can ever say in words and I think perhaps you love me a little.'

'I .. love you with .. all of me,' Giselda answered. 'I love you with my .. heart .. my mind .. my soul .. there is no one in the whole world but .. you.'

Her words seemed to vibrate on the air and the Earl drew her close again and his kisses were more passionate and almost fierce in their intensity.

Giselda felt as if the whole universe was filled with music and with a light that came from Heaven itself.

She had no idea that the touch of the Earl could evoke sensations which she had not known existed and that his arms around her could make her feel safe from everything, even fear.

Her love for him seemed to invade her whole body like a warm tide.

'I love you .. I love you.' she heard herself murmur against his lips.

Then he was kissing her eyes, he cheeks, the tip of her small nose and the softness of her neck.

She knew she aroused him and she wished she could die at this moment when they were so close that it was difficult to believe that they were two people, but had become one.

'I did not know that any woman could be so adorable, so utterly desirable, and at the same time so sweet, so unspoilt, so perfect in every way,' the Earl said in his deep voice.

His lips lingered on the softness of her skin. Then he said quietly :

'How soon will you marry me, my darling?'

To his surprise he felt Giselda stiffen. Then somehow, he was not certain how it happened, she was free of his arms and had moved away from him.

His words had broken the spell which held her, the spell which had made her forget everything but her love and the fact that he loved her.

Now, as if a glass of cold water had been thrown in her face, she was back to reality and in a voice which strove for control she said:

'I .. have something to .. tell you.'

The Earl smiled.

'Your secrets? They are not important, my precious one. All that matters is that you love me. You love me enough to risk your own life to save mine. I am not interested in anything else you may have to say. You are you, and it is you I want for my own, to be with me and beside me for the rest of our lives.'

He saw tears come into her eyes and looking at him she said very softly:

'Could any man be more wonderful .. more magnificent?'

The Earl held out his arms again.

'Come here!' he said. 'I cannot bear you not to be close to me.'

Giselda shook her head.

'You have been standing long enough. You must sit down, and I have to .. talk to you .. even though it is .. hard.'

'Are words so important?' the Earl asked.

But he knew by the expression on her face that she meant what she said. Because he thought it would please her and also because his leg was indeed aching a little, he sat down in an armchair.

Once again he held out his arms in a gesture towards Giselda.

She went towards him but when she reached his chair

she knelt down beside it and raising herself against his knees looked up into his face.

'I love you,' she said. 'I love you so completely and absolutely that I can think of .. nothing else. Every moment that I have .. been with you has been a joy beyond words. At .. night I have fallen asleep thinking of you .. and sometimes dreamt that you were .. with me.'

'That is where I always shall be,' the Earl said.

She shook her head slightly and he felt a sudden fear invade him, even though he told himself he was being nonsensical.

'What are you trying to say to me, Giselda?' he asked.

Now there was a different note in his voice as his eyes looked searchingly down into hers.

'I have been .. waiting for this moment,' she said, 'waiting for when I must .. tell you about myself .. but I kept believing .. because I wanted to believe it .. that there was still time .. time to be near you .. time to talk to you .. time to go on loving you .. even though you did not know it.'

'It took me a little time too,' the Earl said, 'to realise that the feelings I had for you were love. I know now, Giselda, that I have never been in love until this moment.'

He smiled before he went on :

'I have been amused, attracted, fascinated and even infatuated by women, but they have never meant to me what you mean. They have never been part of myself so that I have known I must protect and care for them and that I could not live if they were not in my life, as you will be.'

Again he thought there was that almost imperceptible little shake of Giselda's head and fiercely he asked :

'What are you trying to tell me?'

She drew a deep breath and said :

'Will you .. do something if I ask it?'

'I will do anything you ask me,' the Earl replied.

She raised herself a little further and said :

'Will you .. kiss me? Will you hold me close against you .. and when you have kissed me .. I will tell you .. what you have to .. hear.'

The Earl put his arms around her and drew her close cradling her against him as if she were a child. Then his lips came down on hers to hold her completely captive.

He kissed her passionately in a different manner from the way he had kissed her before until the breath came fitfully from between her lips and she felt a flame rising within her to echo the fire she sensed in him.

When finally he raised his head both their hearts were beating violently and he said aggressively as if he defied some unknown fate that made him afraid :

'You are mine! Nothing and nobody shall take you from me! You are mine, my darling, now and for ever!'

For one moment Giselda lay still against him, her eyes looking up into his. Then she moved away from his arms to stand looking at him for a second before she walked behind his chair to put her hands over his eyes.

'I do not want you to .. look at me,' she said. 'I want you to .. listen.'

'I am listening,' the Earl said.

'Then I want you to know that I love you for all eternity .. there will never be .. could never be .. another man in my life .. and I shall think of you every moment and pray with all my heart for your .. happiness.'

Her voice broke on the last word. Then when the Earl would have spoken, he felt her fingers tighten for a moment across his eyes before she said in a very low voice :

'My .. real name is .. Giselda Charlton! My father was Major Maurice .. Charlton .. now you understand.'

The Earl was rigid with astonishment and he felt Giselda take her hands from his eyes.

Then as he tried to collect his thoughts and a second later turned his head to speak to her, he heard the door of the Sitting-Room close softly and knew she had gone.

For a moment he could hardly credit what had happened or what he had heard, but he rose with an effort and walked to the mantelshelf to reach for the bell-pull.

Even as his hand went out towards it the door opened and Henry Somercote came in.

'It is all right. Everything has been done as you told me, Talbot. I paid off the Dun and Julius is on his way to the coast, although God knows the young swine . . .'

He stopped suddenly and looked at the Earl in anxiety.

'What is the matter, Talbot? What has happened?'

'Stop Giselda!' the Earl cried. 'Stop her before she leaves the house!'

'I think she has already left,' Henry Somercote replied. 'As my carriage drew up at the door I thought it was Giselda I saw running down the street, but I was sure I was mistaken.'

'Oh, my God! She has gone and I do not even know where she lives,' the Earl exclaimed.

'What has occurred? Why did she leave like that? Have you quarrelled?'

'Quarrelled?' the Earl repeated in a strange voice. 'She is Maurice Charlton's daughter!'

'Good Heavens!' Henry Somercote exclaimed. 'How did you discover that?'

'She told me so, and that is why she has left me. I must find her, Henry, I must!'

'Of course – and here we have been searching for him all this year – without any success!'

It was true that ever since they had returned to England from Brussels the Officers of the Regiment had done everything in their power to find Maurice Charlton, but he seemed to have disappeared into thin air.

The only hope was that by some lucky chance they would come across some trace of him.

And now incredibly, completely unexpectedly, the Earl had found Charlton's daughter.

It had been a disastrous episode which in retrospect they all realised should never have occurred. But feelings were high and emotions were uppermost immediately before the Battle of Waterloo.

The Officers of the Earl's Regiment were all stationed in the centre of Brussels, and the evenings when they were off duty were spent in amusing themselves in ways that were most skilfully catered for by the Belgian population.

One of the most attractive of the many *poules de luxe* who were only too willing to entertain English Officers, was Marie Louise Riviere who was superior to and indeed far more attractive than the other sisters of her profession.

Almost everybody in the Earl's Regiment knew Marie Louise, and Major Maurice Charlton, who was an Intelligence Officer on Wellington's staff, was no exception.

Charlton was an experienced soldier and getting on towards forty, but a very attractive man.

Everyone liked him and he was exceedingly popular, not only with his brother Officers but also with the rank and file.

The Earl had seen him once or twice in Marie Louise's Salon where she entertained almost every evening and with the capriciousness of a Princess chose as the evening ended who should be honoured to stay behind after the others had left.

The Earl suspected that Charlton was one of her favourites, but he was not sure.

Then on the afternoon of the Eve of Waterloo a patrol on the outskirts of the city arrested a young Belgian who they thought was acting suspiciously.

He admitted to being a servant of Marie Louise and on his person they found a rough map which was identified as one drawn by Wellington himself as a suggested plan for the order of battle.

It was something which had been discussed by him

only with the Commanders of the different Regiments, the Earl amongst them.

The Duke remembered quite clearly having given the sketch after the conference was over into the hands of Maurice Charlton.

The enquiry which ensued had made all those present, including the Earl, feel embarrassed and extremely sorry for the culprit.

Henry Somercote, Wellington's *Aide-de-Camp*, was present, besides two other officers who, like the Earl, were in the same Regiment as Charlton.

He was horrified when the plan was produced, and protested over and over again that he had put it away in a Despatch Box which always stood by the Duke's bed.

The only thing he admitted was that he could not exactly remember whether he had locked the box when he had left the room.

No one else could have had access to it, and when it was brought in it was found to be locked, but the keys were held by Charlton.

There was nothing Wellington could have done at the time, the Earl recalled, but send the Major back to England under armed guard.

He had left within the hour with instructions that he should be taken back to Barracks where he was to await a Court Martial when the troops returned from the battle front.

What happened was not known to the Earl or indeed to the Duke until the Battle of Waterloo was over.

Then they learnt that on arrival in London Maurice Charlton had evaded his guards, escaped from the Barracks and disappeared.

But before they knew this an Orderly who had been wounded in the battle confessed as he was dying that he was responsible for the theft.

He had taken the keys from Charlton's pocket while he

was having a bath, unlocked the Despatch Box, extracted the plan and returned the keys to his master's pocket.

Marie Louise had paid him well, and he had been promised even greater reward if Napoleon found the plan useful.

The Earl, Henry Somercote and every other Officer in the Regiment had returned to England determined to right the wrong, but they could not find Maurice Charlton.

'Where does Giselda live?' Henry Somercote asked now. 'I have a carriage downstairs.'

'I do not know,' the Earl answered.

'You do not know?' Henry echoed.

The Earl shook his head.

'She would never tell me, and I thought that sooner or later she would trust me with the secret I knew she was hiding.'

He put his hand up to his eyes.

'How could I have imagined — how could I have dreamt even for a moment that she was Charlton's daughter?'

'It seems inconceivable,' Henry Somercote agreed.

'Now I understand why she was so poor,' the Earl said. 'We learnt that Charlton had collected his family from his house in London and taken them away with him — he must have run out of money and when he died they were left starving. Oh, God, Henry, we have to find her!'

He tugged at the bell-pull as he spoke and Henry Somercote said:

'I told you I have a carriage outside.'

'I am not ringing for a carriage but for Batley,' the Earl answered.

The door opened as he spoke.

'Batley,' the Earl said in a tone his valet had never heard before, 'I have lost Miss Giselda and I have to find her. I know I told you to make no further enquiries, but have you the slightest idea where she lives?'

Batley hesitated for a moment.

'I obeyed Your Lordship's orders,' he said, 'but as it

happens it was quite by chance that I learnt Miss Giselda's address.'

'You know? Splendid, Batley – I knew I could depend on you! Where is it?'

'It's in a very low part of the town, M'Lord. I happened to see Miss Giselda walking that way and thought it might be dangerous for her if she was not aware of the type of neighbourhood she was in. So I followed her just in case there was any trouble.'

Batley paused to say uncomfortably:

'I saw her go into a house, M'Lord – in a road where no lady should stay.'

'Take us there, Batley! For God's sake, take us there!'

'Are you well enough for all this?' Henry asked with a note of concern in his voice. 'Let Batley and me go and bring her back to you.'

'Do you imagine I could wait here?' the Earl asked sharply.

Henry did not answer him and Batley, picking up the Earl's cape which he had flung on a chair when he came up to the room, put it over his master's shoulders.

The Earl could only go down the stairs more slowly than he would have wished, and by the time he had reached the hall Henry's carriage was outside. The two gentlemen sat inside while Batley perched on the box beside the coachman.

'How can we ever make reparation for what Charlton's family has suffered because we did not trust him?' the Earl asked bitterly.

'The evidence seemed completely conclusive,' Henry Somercote said. 'I remember thinking myself that it was really impossible for him to be innocent or for the plan to have been stolen without his being aware of it.'

'We were wrong,' the Earl said.

'Yes, we were wrong,' Henry agreed with a sigh.

They drove until the Earl saw they were no longer in the newly laid-out part of the town with its fine buildings but were passing along narrow streets where in the doorways of dingy houses there stood some extremely unsavoury-looking characters.

He could not bear to think of Giselda moving amongst such people or of the dangers she might have encountered.

Yet all he was concerned with at the moment was finding her.

Finally after twisting through a labyrinth of lanes almost too narrow to admit the carriage, they drew up outside a dilapidated house which had lost a number of panes of glass from its windows and whose door seemed to hang precariously on its hinges.

Batley descended from the carriage and knocked on the door.

It was opened after some minutes by a slatternly-looking woman who glared at him suspiciously.

'What d'you want?' she asked uncompromisingly.

'We wish to speak to Miss Chart,' Batley said.

'Nice time o'night for gentlemen to be callin'.' the woman said scathingly.

Then as she looked at the Earl and was obviously overcome by his appearance, she said abruptly:

'Back room!'

She jerked her thumb over her shoulder then disappeared through an adjacent door, slamming it noisily behind her.

The narrow passage which held a flight of steep stairs, some with broken boards, smelt of age, dirt, and damp, and the Earl moved behind the stairs to where there was a door.

He knocked and heard a voice murmur something in a tone of alarm. Then the door was opened and he saw two people staring at him with consternation and fear in their eyes.

One was Giselda who must have only just arrived. Her cheeks were still flushed a little with the speed at which she had run home and her hair was blown by the wind.

She was standing beside her mother who was very much like her in appearance except that her hair was grey and her face was lined with suffering and privation.

Neither of the women said anything. Then ignoring Giselda the Earl went to Mrs Charlton and took her hand in his.

'We have been searching for you, Mrs Charlton, for a whole year,' he said. 'We have been trying to find you to tell you that your husband was unjustly accused and was subsequently completely exonerated.'

He felt her hand tremble in his and her eyes looking up searched his face as if for confirmation of his words.

Then in a voice he could hardly hear she asked:

'Is this . . true?'

'Completely true,' the Earl answered, 'and I can only express on behalf of myself, His Grace the Duke of Wellington and the Regiment our deepest and most heart-felt apologies for having brought this sorrow upon you all.'

He paused to say:

'If only your husband had waited! The Duke sent an Officer back to England the moment the battle was over to tell him that his name had been cleared and that the thief confessed the crime before he died.'

Mrs Charlton gave a deep sigh as if the burden she had carried on her shoulders was no longer there. Then she said:

'I am glad for my children's sake, that you discovered the truth, but you . . cannot give me back . . my husband.'

'I am aware of that,' the Earl replied, 'but I think he would be glad that you should no longer suffer on his behalf or hide in shame.'

He still held Mrs Charlton's hand in both of his and now pressing it warmly he said:

'It will be a little comfort to you to know that there is not only your husband's pay and pension waiting for you in London, but there is also quite a considerable sum of money. It was collected by the Officers of the Regiment and subscribed to by the Duke himself and we intended to offer it to the Major as compensation for what he suffered by being unjustly accused.'

He saw the pain in her expression and he added:

'It will be useful to make sure that Rupert gets really strong and well when he is allowed to leave the hospital.'

It was then that the tears came into Mrs Charlton's eyes and the Earl for the first time looked around the room.

He had never seen anything so poor, such an impossible background for the beauty of Giselda: dirty walls with paper peeling from them, rotten floorboards, and three iron bedsteads which were practically the only furniture.

Making up his mind quickly and with an authority of manner, which those who served with him knew meant he intended to have his own way, the Earl said:

'I have a carriage outside and I am taking you both away from here at this moment!'

For the first time he looked directly at Giselda.

'This is no fit place for you,' he said, 'as you well know.'

She did in fact look very out of place in her beautiful pink gown, the room in contrast seeming even more unpleasant than it might have seemed if she had been differently dressed.

Henry Somercote was speaking to Mrs Charlton.

'I would like to tell you, Ma'am,' he said, 'how fond we all were of your husband and how desperately concerned we were when we learnt that he had disappeared.'

She could not answer him because of her tears, but he went on:

'The Earl has been ill, but I personally have travelled to many parts of England this past year hoping to find some trace of Maurice.'

'He was always .. proud of the Regiment,' Mrs Charlton managed to say.

'It was a terrible misunderstanding,' Henry replied sympathetically.

The Earl was close to Giselda.

'How could you leave me?' he asked in a low voice. 'How could you imagine that whoever you were I would have let you go?'

'I tried to .. hate you, as I hated all those who did not .. believe in my father,' she answered.

'But you failed,' the Earl said softly.

She looked at him, and seeing in her eyes how much she loved him he knew that nothing would ever separate them again in the future.

'You belong to me,' he said softly so that no one else could hear.

7

The Earl allowed Batley to help him into bed and lay back against the pillows.

'As it seems to have turned cold this evening, M'Lord,' Batley said, 'I've taken the liberty of lighting the fire, only a small one, but there's a wind coming from the Malvern Hills which will grow colder during the night.'

'I am sure that is very sensible, Batley,' the Earl replied.

The valet picked up His Lordship's evening clothes and turned towards the door.

'I just wish to say, M'Lord, it's been a very happy day and I wishes you and Her Ladyship all the best for the rest of your lives together.'

'Thank you, Batley.'

The door closed behind the valet and the Earl waited.

It had in fact been a long day and there had been a great deal to do in the previous two days since he and Henry had taken Mrs Charlton and Giselda away from the slum in which they had been living.

That night they had stayed as the Colonel's guests at German Cottage but the following morning the Earl had been determined to find them comfortable apartments where Mrs Charlton could look after Rupert when he came out of hospital.

They found exactly what the Earl thought adequate in the recently completed Royal Crescent.

They had become the tenants of a beautifully decorated suite on the first floor consisting of two comfortable bedrooms and a large Sitting-Room.

The Earl was quite certain Mrs Charlton would soon be receiving a number of friends who, once they knew she was at Cheltenham would be only too pleased to renew their acquaintance with her.

Giselda had stayed for two nights with her mother in Royal Crescent spending the days buying for her clothes and many luxuries they had thought she would never see again.

When she learnt of the large sum of money that had been collected for her father, Giselda found it almost impossible to express her gratitude.

'If only we had known,' she whispered at length.

'If only we had been able to find you,' the Earl answered.

He had learnt by then of some of the privations and miseries that the family had suffered after Major Charlton had taken them away from London the night he had escaped his guards.

He had known his house would be the first place they would look for him, so they had hastily bundled together everything they could and having hired a carriage they had driven from London into the country.

Maurice Charlton, who was quite a resourceful man, was determined to find work but the difficulty was that he had no references, and apart from being a soldier he had few qualifications.

Finally he had worked on a farm looking after the horses about which he was quite an expert, but unfortunately while he had been doing so he had been tossed and gored by a bull.

This was why as the Earl could now understand, Giselda was so expert at bandaging.

An inexperienced country doctor and their inability to pay for better treatment made Maurice Charlton's wounds heal slowly, and finally he developed pneumonia.

Almost before his wife and daughter realised what was happening he had died.

'I do not think he wished to live,' Giselda said passionately when she told the Earl what had happened. 'He was so ashamed and humiliated that the men he thought to be his friends did not believe him.'

Her voice was bitter as she continued:

'He had always been a man of honour, a man of his word. Even as children we were severely punished if we told even the smallest falsehood.'

'I know it seems very hard, my darling,' the Earl said soothingly, 'but circumstances were very strong against him. He was the only person who had the key, the only person the Duke entrusted with his secret papers.'

'If he had not .. associated with .. that woman perhaps it would never have happened,' Giselda said in a hard little voice.

The Earl realised that her father had confessed to his wife and daughter his association with Marie Louise.

He thought perhaps this would have hurt Giselda more than anything else. Children are always very intolerant of their parents' weaknesses.

Because he had no desire to discuss it, he asked:

'Tell me what happened after your father died.'

'Mama thought that Rupert should go to school .. even a school where one paid as little as a penny a day would be better than no education at all.'

Giselda sighed as she went on:

'She worked all the time on her embroidery and because she sewed so beautifully I found everything she made was easy to sell. The shops paid us very little but charged their customers quite enormous sums.'

'So you came to Cheltenham?'

'We found lodgings outside the town in a village,' Giselda replied, 'and we were really quite comfortable. Then Rupert was knocked down by a Phaeton.'

The Earl saw the horror in her face and heard it in the tone of her voice and he put his arms around her.

'That is something else you will have to forget, my

precious,' he said. 'Newell tells me that Rupert will be walking quite normally in another six months. Until then I intend to engage a Tutor for him, and after that, if he still needs treatment, I shall arrange a holiday for him and your mother at one of the Spas in Europe.'

'You are so kind .. so very, very kind,' Giselda murmured.

The Earl had already told her that he intended to give Mrs Charlton a house on the estate at Lynd Park.

'There are several charming small manors to choose from or the Dower House if your mother would pefer it. They will be near us and I think your mother and Rupert will make many congenial friends in the immediate neighbourhood.'

The Earl paused to say gently :

'But I shall be jealous if you spend too much time with your family and neglect me.'

'You know I would never do that,' Giselda protested. 'Never, never! I want to be with you! I want to be close to you .. every moment .. as I have always wanted to be.'

She gave a wistful little smile as she added :

'You do not know how much I resented having to be with Julius when I might have been with you. I knew that you had planned the part I should play as much to help me as to save him, but I much preferred being .. your servant!'

'My Nurse – my guide – my inspiration, and my love!' the Earl corrected.

She put her cheek against his in a manner that was even more tender than if she had kissed him, and he thought that he had never known a woman who could make such endearing gestures.

He found that the look in Giselda's eyes and the lilt in her voice could tell him of her love as eloquently as words and she made him want her more and more every hour that passed.

'You are not really well enough to get married,' Giselda had protested when the Earl planned their wedding for the third day after the drama in the theatre.

'I cannot wait any longer,' he said masterfully. 'I have lost you once and I am taking no further chances. You will marry me here in Cheltenham and we will leave the following day for Lynd Park.'

When Giselda would have argued he put his finger on her lips and continued:

'Later, when I'm really well, I am going to take you abroad, but for the moment I think we will both be content to be together in the country.'

'It would not matter to me if it was in a coal-mine or on the moon, just as long as I can be with you,' Giselda answered.

'Until you get bored with me,' the Earl teased.

'Do you really think I could ever do that?' she asked. 'It is much more likely that you will become bored with me. You do not like stupid women, but you dislike it when I argue.'

'I love everything you do,' the Earl said positively.

He had pulled her to him and turned her face up to his.

'I have never, and this is the truth, Giselda,' he said quietly, 'known anything so perfect or so exciting as your lips. They thrill me as I have never been thrilled before.'

'Is . . that really . . true?'

He answered her by kissing her until there was a flush on her cheeks and her eyes were shining like stars.

When he released her he said hoarsely:

'If you imagine I can wait one moment after tomorrow to make you my wife you are very much mistaken. I am well now, my darling, well enough to show you how much I love you.'

At the passion in his voice she hid her face against his shoulder and he kissed her hair. Then he touched it gently with his fingers and said:

'Tomorrow night I shall see this falling over your shoulders and I shall know how long it is. I have always wondered.'

·   ·   ·   ·   ·   ·

They were married very quietly in St Mary's, the Parish Church since the twelfth century.

Colonel Berkeley was Best Man and there were only Mrs Charlton and Captain Somercote as witnesses.

'If we invite one other person we shall have to invite the lot!' the Earl said, 'and I have always loathed the idea of being a "Peep Show" simply because I am being married to someone I love.'

The Church which had been built in the shape of a Cross was filled with lilies which scented the air, and it seemed to Giselda that there was something very sacred in the vows they made to each other.

She knew that they would withstand all the difficulties and problems of time and their love and joy in each other would only deepen as the years passed.

The Earl insisted, although Giselda said it was an extravagance, on her having a white wedding gown, and Madame Vivienne had made her look the embodiment of beauty which was the ideal of all brides.

Her veil was one of the finest lace which might have been made by fairy fingers and it fell over the gown of white gauze trimmed with the same lace.

Her wreath was not of orange blossoms but of white roses just in bud, and she carried a bouquet of the same flowers.

She was given away by Henry Somercote but the Earl had said to her :

'I know the Duke would be only too pleased to take your father's place if we asked him.'

'I would rather have someone in your Regiment,'

Giselda answered, 'and I think Captain Somercote was really fond of Papa.'

'That is true,' the Earl agreed. 'Henry did more than anyone else to try to find your father.'

'Then I would like him to give me away,' Giselda said and added softly '. . to you.'

When she came up the aisle on Henry's arm the Earl thought it would be impossible for anyone to look more lovely or more pure.

He knew he had found in Giselda what he had always missed in the other women he had known.

Granted they had been sophisticated, Society beauties, but in his heart he had thought that the ideals which his mother had implanted in him as a child could only materialise in a woman whose character and personality were pure and untouched by sin.

Everything Giselda had ever done, he realised, was selfless, and if she had tried to sacrifice herself it was for others, while he who had always been courageous admired and respected her courage.

It was difficult to tell her what he felt when he knew she had saved his life by an action which might have destroyed her own.

She had acted out of love and he knew that it came from a heart filled with love which she gave not only to him but to everyone who suffered.

He realised exactly what she had felt for poor Emily Clutterbuck.

He understood how instinctively she disliked deceiving Julius and tried to find the best in him.

In fact Giselda was everything he believed a woman should be, and he knew as he took his marriage vows that he was fortunate as few men were privileged to be.

To Giselda her marriage was something which came from Heaven itself.

Loving the Earl and supposing that she could never mean anything in his life had been a pain and a happiness, an agony and an ecstasy that even now she could hardly believe had become the rapture of requited love.

The night before her wedding she had prayed for a long time beside her bed.

She thanked God that her father's name had been cleared and thanked Him that in His inscrutable and mysterious way He had brought the Earl into her life.

She was grateful in a manner that could never be expressed in words that he loved her as she had longed for him to do.

How could she ever have imagined, she asked herself, when she was sent upstairs to clean the grate in a guest's bedroom, that the guest would be in her father's Regiment; a man who she began to love almost from the moment she met him?

She had known on the night the Earl engaged her that if she did what she felt to be right she would leave German Cottage and disappear.

But she had learnt the hard way that jobs were difficult to find, and she was afraid that if she gave up what seemed a lucrative position she might never find another one.

In which case, she argued with her conscience, Mama would starve to death and Rupert would never walk again.

Instinctively, because she was sensitive, Giselda had known there was a compelling, exciting and irresistible magnetism between herself and the Earl that she could not express in words, but nevertheless was irrefutably there.

She had known it as her footsteps quickened in the morning when she went to his room and when she returned from any errands on which he had sent her.

She had known from the pain in her breast when she must say goodnight and knew that many hours must pass before she could see him again.

Her love was a secret she held in her breast, and yet the wonder of it permeated her whole being so that she felt as if she became a new personality!

She had become someone who could touch the stars even while in contrast she knew when her love was no longer there she would go down into the darkest bowels of the earth.

'We have so many things to do together,' she told herself now, 'and I will take care of him and make him happy with a happiness he has never really known because he has been alone.'

The Earl was thinking very much the same as he waited with two candles alight beside the big four-poster, and the fire flickering fitfully in the grate.

There was the fragrance of roses and carnations on the air but the shadows were dark.

He began to be half-afraid that Giselda would not come to him and yet he knew that she would not expect him to come to her bedroom.

The suite in German Cottage consisted of the best room which he had always used but which ordinarily would have been the perquisite of a woman.

The smaller bedroom on the other side of the Sitting-Room where Mrs Kingdom had now moved Giselda's things had really been planned as the gentleman's dressing-room.

'She will come to me,' the Earl told himself.

Then as he waited, his heart beating in anticipation the door opened and Giselda came in.

As she moved very slowly towards him he saw that she was looking just as he had wished her to look with her fair hair falling over her shoulders to just below her waist.

She was wearing a white négligée and her cheeks were very pale but her eyes were large and soft with love.

She came slowly nearer and nearer to the bed. Then she said in a voice which told the Earl she was nervous:

'You are quite .. comfortable? You are not in .. pain because you .. stood for so .. long today?'

'Batley has looked after me as you told him to do,' the

Earl replied. 'He put me to bed like a baby when I am now quite capable of looking after myself.'

'I will . . look after . . you in . . future.'

'As I will look after you.'

She stood by the bed and after a moment he said:

'It is embarrassing for you, my darling, having to come to me when I should come to you, but there seemed no alternative.'

'I wanted to come,' Giselda said, 'but now I do not know . . quite what to . . do.'

'What do you want to do?' the Earl asked.

Her eyes met his in the light of the candles and she said in a voice he could hardly hear:

'I . . want to be . . close to you.'

'You cannot want it more than I do, my precious.'

She drew a little breath as if that was what she wished to hear, then he saw the radiance in her face as she bent forward and blew out the candles.

Her négligée slipped to the ground and for a moment the Earl saw her body silhouetted through her diaphanous nightgown against the glow of the flames.

Then two strong arms drew her into the bed.

The Earl held her very tight. He could feel that she was trembling, and her heart was beating as frantically as his.

'I love you! Oh, my darling, precious little wife, I love you! Now we are together, as I have always wanted us to be.'

'Together . .' Giselda whispered, 'b . but I am afraid you will be . . disappointed because you hate . . thin women.'

The Earl laughed and turned her face up to his.

'If you were as fat as an elephant or as thin as a pin I should still love you. But as it is no one could be so soft, adorable and unbelievably beautiful.'

His lips were on hers, then she felt him slipping her nightgown from her shoulders and he kissed her neck and then her breasts until she moved even closer to him.

'I love you! God, how I love you!' he said. 'How could I have known that the mysterious maid-servant I first met in this room would one day lie close against me like this? You make me feel the proudest and most fortunate man in the whole world.'

'You said I was to .. remain in your .. employment until you .. no longer had .. need of me,' Giselda murmured.

'That will not be until the stars fall from the Heavens and the world no longer exists,' the Earl replied. 'I shall always need you, Giselda, in this world and the world beyond. You are mine! You are part of me and we can never be free of each other.'

'I .. would not .. wish it any other .. way,' she whispered. 'I want .. only you and nothing else in the world is of the least .. importance.'

There was a little throb of passion in her voice which moved the Earl tremulously.

Then his lips were on hers and he was kissing her until there was no need for words, and everything in the world vanished except themselves.

They became one person.

There were no more mysteries, no more secrets, only love – a love stretching out towards an indefinable horizon.